Letters to Elise

CODA STERLING

ISBN: 978-1-959008-54-5

Chapter
One

Ivy Stonewall tried not to cry. She couldn't save all of them. With the end-of-project bonus money she had, she'd be doing good if she could rescue one or two.

The horses, yellow numbers on their hindquarters, stood crowded together in pens. Most of them were young and in reasonable condition. A few were thin, angular hips giving way to protruding ribs. Many had their heads down. They might not know exactly what was happening to them, but they seemed to suspect that something bad was coming. Rescues would pick up some. A few more would find private owners.

Most would go to slaughter.

It's too hard to decide. They all deserve a chance. She looked from pinched, white-rimmed eyes to the dull eyes of the ones who had already given up, her heart breaking.

Her friend Julie, who helped her run the Copper Penny Horse Rescue, approached, scrawling on a notepad.

"I think I found a couple of good candidates. They were at a horse camp for kids. They should be easy to adopt out, and we might get enough money to keep the others in grain for the next month or so."

Ivy nodded. At the far end of the feedlot, a horse stood alone, separated from the others.

"Did you look at that one?"

"No. I think it may be quarantined."

Ivy couldn't help herself. Her feet started taking her in the direction of the lone animal.

Julie put her fists on her hips, her dark curly hair bouncing as she strode after Ivy. "Where are you going?"

"Just to check it out. Be right back."

"Ivy..."

The horse raised its head as she approached. Ivy hadn't realized how big it was—its withers were taller than her, so she estimated 17 hands. She had to guess, because the animal was on the far side of the pen, and she couldn't go inside. Ivy used the pipe fencing as her height guide.

Thick yellow mucus oozed from the horse's nose, and it wheezed with every breath. Ivy bent to take a peek under its belly. *Mare.* She looked like a draft horse cross—big-boned, tall, and well-muscled, but she was a piebald. Most drafts don't come in black and white swirls. She was a few hundred pounds underweight, although her abdomen was distended. *I bet she's in foal—either that or she's got a massive parasite load.* Ivy shook her head. The mare regarded her with bright eyes, one blue, the other brown, but she made no move to approach.

Scars crisscrossed the horse's quarters. *Whip marks.* The long black and white mane was in a hopeless tangle, and it appeared to have been some time since she'd last had her hooves trimmed.

Julie came up behind her. "No. Ivy? No. Don't you see all that snot? It's probably got strangles. You can't bring it to the rescue. I've found two healthy horses we should be able to adopt out quickly. This one is a massive vet bill, and it may not even live."

The mare's bulging abdomen twitched.

"She's pregnant."

Julie's lips tightened. "Oh, good. I was just thinking I've been getting way too much sleep lately and I should bottle-feed an orphan foal or something."

"Look at her face. I can't…" Ivy shook her head slowly.

Julie sighed and threw her hands in the air. "Fine. Let's go find Tom and see if he'll sell her outright. I wish you'd listen to me, though. We could save multiple horses for what she'll cost in vet bills."

Ivy closed her eyes for a moment and swallowed. "I know you're right. But there's something in her eyes…. I can't leave her." They started toward Tom's office. "I'll bet he wants her gone before the state inspector shows up—he isn't going to spend the time or money to properly quarantine her and disinfect the pens."

"That big ole' black and white mare? You sure you want her? She's sick."

Ivy licked her lips. "We know."

"Well, if you haul her off, it'll save me a couple of shells and some gasoline. But you have to take her tonight. Fifty bucks for the feed I already put into her."

That's the most expensive three flakes of hay ever. Ivy took an envelope from her purse and counted out two twenties and a ten. "Thank you, Tom."

He smiled at the money, his bony fingers folding the bills in half before he stuffed them into his pocket. "You rescue people are crazy." The reflections of the flickering fluorescent light on his bald head made Ivy think of melted ice cream as she turned to leave.

Julie pulled the trailer up to the loading area while Ivy went to see about getting someone to bring the mare. *I sure hope she fits. Otherwise, Tom will take her out back and shoot her.*

"Mason?" *Where is that idiot wrangler?*

As Ivy walked up and down the dimly lit aisles, she called to Tom's helper. But he was nowhere to be found. When she rounded the outer corner, her heart fell.

She couldn't see the big mare in her pen.

Had she collapsed? Did Mason put her on the auction floor, after all? Surely not, given that she was sick. Ivy's mind raced as she power-walked to the isolated stall. The gate was ajar, and there was no horse.

Her stomach lurched. *Where is she?*

She didn't want to run and alarm the horses standing shoulder to shoulder in their small pens, but she was in a terrible hurry. She compromised by keeping her arms at her sides as she half-jogged back to the trailer.

There! Mason was leading the mare into the pen with the loading chute. Relief washed over Ivy, followed by a current of unease. *Is she even going to fit through that?*

As they neared the narrow passage, the horse stopped and raised her head, her breath wheezing more loudly with each exertion. She snorted, and a massive wad of mucus splattered into the dirt. Mason's leathery skin hardly moved as his thin lips parted to let a growl escape. He yanked at the lead rope. She didn't budge. The mare outweighed him by a lot, so there was no chance he could brute force her into that chute.

"Let me help." Ivy put on as friendly a smile as she could muster.

He spat tobacco juice on the ground. "This is a great big horse. I don't want you to get hurt—leave it to the professionals."

Ivy wanted to slap the smirk off his ugly mouth, but she gritted her teeth instead. "It might be easier to just load her straight into the trailer—that chute is designed for cows, not big horses. Can she even squeeze through there?"

Julie hopped out of the truck to see what was taking so long and stood next to Ivy, her eyes darting from Mason to the horse and back again.

"You want to load the horses, you get a job here." Mason again tugged on the lead. The mare took a step backward.

Mason twirled the end of the rope to hit her on the haunches. Quicker than he could notice and take evasive action, the horse pinned her ears and grabbed his arm in her teeth. She shook him like a terrier shakes a rat and flung him against the side of the corral. He went down hard. The horse turned her quarters to him and raised a threatening hoof.

Ivy and Julie looked at each other, then jumped the fence. As they ran into the pen, Ivy said, "I'll deal with him. You get her on the trailer, any way you can, as fast as you can."

Julie took the mare, and Ivy crouched over Mason. Blood seeped through his torn sleeve. "Are you okay?"

Mason sat up and let out a string of profanity that would make a sailor blush.

A series of loud, echoing bangs came from the direction of the trailer. *That mare had better be loading up and not destroying anything.*

"Do you have a first-aid kit? Can I help?"

Clutching his arm, the man struggled to his feet. "I'm going for the shotgun. That damned horse is dead."

Ivy froze, parsing his words. *Horse is dead...is dead... dead.* The impact of that single syllable hit her like a bullet, and she sprinted across the pen. Julie was just closing the trailer door. "Go! Go! Go!"

They handed their paperwork to the gate guard and were on the road before Mason made it out of the office with the gun. His figure, fist raised, shrank in the side mirror as Julie floored it, the engine whining under the strain.

She rolled her eyes. "Fantastic choice, Ivy."

Jax Carter ran his palm along the old horse's back before he leaned down and started scrubbing between the forelegs with the rubber curry mitt. Joints crackling, the gelding stretched his head up and worked his lips, flapping them together and curling his top lip.

"Still the best sweet spot, huh, Murph?"

The horse twisted his head around and closed his eyelids, enjoying the grooming. White hairs now frosted his chocolate brown face, and the hollows above his eyes had deepened to pits. Jax used the mitt to scour off the shedding hair. Murphy dropped his head, muzzle just above the ground, his eyes half shut.

Jax checked his watch. "Your food's soaked long enough."

He stepped out of the stall and retrieved a rubber tub of alfalfa pellets that had disintegrated in a warm water bath. The horse's teeth were so worn down that he couldn't chew well, and soaking the food did most of the work for him. His ears flicked toward the tub, and he buried his nose in his meal. Jax gave him another pat and left him to go eat his own dinner.

Fluorescent lights over the receptionist's desk dimly lit the waiting area, but there was no one in the veterinarian's front office. It was a busy equine practice, and the clinic was manned twenty-four hours, although at night there was a skeleton crew who would be treating horses, mucking stalls, and assisting the on-call doctors with any emergencies.

Jax peered over the counter. "Hello? Delta?"

There was no reply. He tried the door that led back to the surgery and exam rooms, but it was locked. That left him little choice but to wait. Someone would come to the desk eventually, and Delta knew he would be stopping by. He'd called earlier and ordered some senior joint supplement for Murphy—his schedule had been crazy lately and this was the first chance he'd had to pick it up. Jax slouched in a well-used chair, legs stretched out in front of him, and checked email on his phone.

He didn't have to idle in the lobby too long. The throaty rattle of a diesel engine sounded from the back driveway, the one that led to the quarantine barn. The truck got louder, then stopped. Doors slammed. Voices. Jax decided to go outside and tell the staffer he was there.

As he pulled the door open, someone else had started to push it. That someone came stumbling in, and he reached out to catch them. He suddenly found a young woman with wide brown eyes in his arms.

"Sorry. Are you okay?" He set her back on her feet.

She let out a breath. "Yeah. Sure. I wasn't expecting the door to open itself."

"Stop!" Delta broke into the awkward moment as she came into the lobby from the clinic entrance. "Take off your shoes. And use this before you touch anything." She squirted a couple of globs of hand sanitizer onto the other woman's palms. "Ivy Stonewall, you know better than to track God-knows-what from that auction around my clinic." A silver-streaked wisp of black hair slipped out of the clip at the back of her head.

Ivy nodded and slipped off her boots, then rubbed the gel over her hands and up her forearms. "Excuse me."

She hurried off to the ladies' room.

Jax watched her leave, admiring the view. "Auction?"

"Yes. She and her friend run the Copper Penny Horse Rescue. They picked up a doozy tonight. Pregnant draft with a bad upper respiratory infection. Come on over to the desk—I've got that tub for you."

Jax followed her across the lobby. She pulled a plastic pail of supplement out from under the counter, and he handed her his credit card. Ivy exited the restroom and came over to stand nearby.

She looked at his purchase. "Old horse?"

He nodded.

She smiled. "Good for you. Hardly anybody wants to take care of the elderly. I have two myself."

Delta gave Jax his card back and turned to Ivy. "We'll culture that snot and get her on some antibiotics. Dr. Clark'll probably lance those lymph nodes and palpate to see how far along he thinks the foal is. Mare's a bit dehydrated from the fever, so we'll run some fluids on her tonight."

Ivy sighed, took an envelope out of her purse, and handed it to Delta, who wrote something on it and tucked it into the drawer.

"Thanks. Call me as soon as you know anything."

Delta nodded. "I have treatments to do, so…"

"Later." Ivy turned to leave.

Jax smiled at Delta and followed Ivy. He held the door open for her as she slipped her shoes back on. She wasn't classically beautiful. Her hair was a mess and her smile was a little lopsided, but there was a softness, a warmth about her that Jax found appealing. He glanced at her left hand. Nothing.

"So. You run a horse rescue, is that right?"

"Did Delta tell you that?"

Jax nodded.

Ivy's smile brightened. "She sometimes gives me a hard time about going to the auctions, but you should ask her how many horses she has at home that were abandoned at the clinic."

"Easy to imagine. My name is Jax, by the way."

The driver of the truck honked—two quick taps.

"I have to go. Julie's got a schedule to keep." She pulled out her cell phone and opened the wallet-style cover, then handed him a business card. "We can always use volunteers at the Copper Penny."

Was that an invitation to call her, or to come muck out stalls? "Cool."

He shoved the card into his shirt pocket, wondering if it was an opportunity, a liability, or just a piece of paper.

Chapter
Two

JULIE SHIFTED THE truck into gear. "Who was that?"

Ivy shrugged. "Some guy. Said his name was Jax."

"Some guy, huh? Because you always hand out your cards to random men."

Who are you? My mother? "He was getting stuff for his geriatric horse. Seemed like the kind of guy who might be willing to volunteer at the rescue."

"I see." Julie winced as they hit a pothole and the empty trailer rattled behind them. "It doesn't hurt that he looks like he stepped out of a firefighter calendar."

Ivy felt the heat rising up her neck and onto her cheeks, so she looked out the window. "There's nothing wrong with improving the scenery at the barn."

The vibration of her phone in her pocket made her jump. *Has Doctor Clark already looked at our mare? That was awfully quick.* She didn't recognize the number, but it could be someone asking for help with a horse.

"Hello?"

"Hey, Baby Girl."

Ivy didn't try to conceal her indignant sigh. "What do you want, Chance?" She couldn't help searching nearby traffic for his red truck.

Julie scowled from the driver's seat.

"I just wanted to hear your voice. I miss you, girl."

"You should have thought about that before you started screwing around. Are you drunk?"

"Nah. Just a beer or two. I'm at Casey's if you want to come down and shoot some pool. Be like old times."

"No. Quit calling me. The divorce was final last year. Nothing is going to change that. Goodbye, Chance."

She ended the call and then immediately blocked the number. "Men suck."

Julie eased onto the highway. "Don't let that douche canoe get you down. There are some great guys out there. At least that's what my mother keeps telling me."

Ivy almost laughed. Julie's mom was always trying to set her up with a 'nice young man.' For all the good it would do. Julie had been dating Karen for almost two years, and things were getting pretty serious. If her mother suspected they were more than just roommates, she didn't let on.

Julie checked her mirror. "How are we doing on hay?"

They talked rescue business most of the way to the car wash. Fund-raising was always the biggest issue, and the envelope with $1,150 that Ivy had just given to Delta was probably only a down payment on the vet bill, even with the massive rescue discount the clinic gave them.

"Did you realize that the Salt River Group is doing their charity contest again this year?" Julie asked. "They've bumped the prize up to $10,000 for the top ten charities. Each."

"Lucky for us, they need a big tax deduction. We were so close last year. Maybe we should try again?"

"Already entered us and posted the link on all our socials."

Julie eased the truck through the car wash stall so that the trailer was in the prime hosing location. Most people didn't want to get out of their cars and use the pressure wand, so typically, this place wasn't very busy. A dose of hot soapy water, followed by a good bleach spray back at the house, should kill off any nasty bugs lurking in the trailer.

After they were done, they headed back to Ivy's place. She had a twenty-acre plot of land with an aging double-wide trailer just off the edge of the sprawling city. All the rescue horses lived there as well, except for a handful of fosters, which lived offsite.

Once the trailer was disinfected, the horses were checked on, and Julie was on her way to meet Karen, Ivy showered and collapsed on the sofa. It was late, and she was exhausted, but her mind was whirling ninety to nothing. *Was the mare going to be okay? Would the baby survive? What would she do with two draft horses?* Ivy turned her head to look out the window and caught a whiff of cologne. She mentally retraced her steps to the vet clinic. *That Jax guy was pretty hot. Will he call?*

"Oh, no," she said to the two dogs curled at her feet. "I need another man in my life like I need a hole in my head."

Jax sat at the polished marble bar, a craft beer in front of him. Colorful abstract canvases—painted by the elephants at the Houston Zoo, the sign said—hung between arched picture windows. Even though it was summer, half the skinny-jeans-clad males in this place were wearing knitted hats. If it were up to him, he'd never set foot in here. But it wasn't. It was Helen's idea, and whatever Helen wanted, Helen usually got.

"There you are!" called a blonde woman. Younger than he, she opened her arms as she approached and threw them around his neck. He returned the embrace.

She pulled away and gave him an air kiss near his cheek, then she turned and beckoned to the two men who had followed her over.

"André, this is my brother, Ajax." She turned to Jax. "André is the vice president of public affairs for the Salt River Group. He's organizing the kickoff gala for the charity contest, and he wants committee members from all the participating charities."

"Everybody calls me Jax." He extended his hand to the newcomer. "Except for Helen."

André's smile was sympathetic. "I, too, have siblings. Your delightful sister has been telling me about your children's literacy charity. I wish you good luck."

"Thank you. BookStar can use every resource we can get."

His brother-in-law, Morgan Butterfield, tugged him into a more-than-a-handshake-less-than-a-hug greeting. He hated when his BIL did that because it felt more like one-upmanship than genuine affection. So, when Morgan pulled him, he resisted. It was the other man who had to take a half-step forward to rebalance himself. *Why does he even try this anymore?* Jax curled heavier weights than Morgan's body mass at least three days a week in the weight room. Something dark flickered across his eyes before he grinned and clapped Jax on the back.

"We hardly ever see you, Jax. You should come for brunch on Sunday."

Morgan knew that Jax usually worked on Sundays, and certainly would be this weekend, with the big music festival in town.

"I'll have my people call your people."

His brother-in-law gave him a blank look, followed by the fakest smile Jax had ever seen. "Excuse me."

Morgan stepped over to André, presumably to offer his opinion on the best cocktail order.

Jax looked at his sister. Helen was in her element—she'd always relished being the queen bee in high school and never given up that role. She'd married well, and enjoyed her life as a socialite and charity fund-raising maven. He wasn't crazy about Morgan, but Helen had the life she wanted and seemed happy enough.

By the end of the evening, Jax had been commandeered onto the Welcoming Committee. He didn't mind. BookStar needed all the visibility it could get. Donations hadn't exactly been pouring in lately. *I'll have to get Helen on it*. He smiled to himself.

Jax had left the kitchen light on, so the house wasn't completely dark. He shucked off his boots at the back door, and his border collie mix dog, Flip, met him there, lazily wagging his tail. He took the dog out for a potty break.

Only the brightest stars were visible against the charcoal grey sky, but he picked out the Big Dipper and Polaris while Flip sniffed around for just the right spot to pee. When the dog's mission was accomplished, Jax gave the stars one last look as he closed the front door. A shooting star arced across the sky. He felt he should wish for something, but he wasn't sure what.

As he got undressed, the business card from the Copper Penny Horse Rescue fell out of his shirt pocket. He picked it up and studied it for a moment. Ivy Stonewall, what is it you really want from me? What would you say if I called you? Come feed horses, or come out to dinner? Probably don't have time to find out right now. If she runs a horse rescue, she probably doesn't have time either. He set the card on the dresser and turned out the light.

Chapter
Three

As usual, Ivy ate her lunch at her desk. It wasn't healthy, according to all the magazines, but those article writers didn't have to make sure they left the office in time to take care of a dozen horses. Two of her rescues were so old that she was always a little surprised when she got home and found them still moving. But they didn't seem to be in any pain, and they enjoyed snoozing together under the trees, so she kept feeding them.

As she put her lunch tote away, the handle caught on one of the magenta African violets that lined the end of her desk like a miniature privacy hedge. She sighed as she picked up the broken leaf. Ivy did not need yet another magenta African violet, but she would put it in dirt and grow a new plant anyway. Maybe she could pawn one off on Martha down the hall.

Ivy punched Dr. Clark's number into her phone. She'd been in a meeting when he'd called earlier.

The day manager answered the phone.

"Hey, Ivy. Dr. Clark is in surgery right now, but I can give you an update on your girl. The labs haven't all come back yet—the bacterial culture will probably be finished tomorrow. She is negative on the Coggins. A little anemic, white count's way up, just like you'd expect for a bacterial infection. Dr. Mueller palpated her, and she thinks the foal is probably around nine months along."

"So, two more months then."

"If she doesn't drop it early from all the stress. Dr. Mueller did drain those abscesses. At least she can breathe without squeaking now. She was able to eat a little bit of grain, now that she can swallow."

"Thanks, Mary. I'll be out this evening after work to see her."

"Alrighty. Delta'll be here at eight."

A man poked his head into Ivy's cubicle. "Ivy, did you get a chance to—Oh, sorry."

"I have to go, Mary. Thanks for the update." She hung up and turned toward her boss, Vern Thompson. Her eyes dropped to her to-do list. "Did I have a chance to update that Gantt chart? Yes, I did."

"Great. Could you print it for me right quick? I'm on the way to a meeting with the VPs." Anyone else would look for it on the network drive, but Vern was a technophobe and didn't trust PowerPoint. Ivy would have to pry his printed handouts from his cold, dead fingers.

"Sure. I'll send it to the printer on the third floor. Six?"

He nodded and hurried away.

Ivy's interrupt-driven day continued as per normal, and when 4:30 finally rolled around, she struggled to keep herself from running out to the bus stop. Unless there was an accident in the HOV lane, the express bus took less than half the time to get her to the Park and Ride lot as it would take for her to drive. It was another fifteen minutes from there to her house. She used her time on the bus to answer emails, do research, and read a book.

She was halfway home when she got a text from Julie. "OMG. Where are you?"

"Bus."

"Just picked up mail. You have to see this."

A moment later, a photo of a letter followed. Ivy read it and texted Julie back.

"They want us on the Welcoming Committee for the kick-off gala? Wow."

"A representative. You."

"Don't you want to?"

"Nope. Karen and I are in the Caymans that week."

All I need now is a fairy godmother to whip me up a ball-worthy dress. "K"

Ivy looked at the letter again. As a committee member, she and a guest were entitled to attend the gala for free. *Maybe the FG can arrange a date, too.* The image of the guy from the vet clinic flickered across her mind, but she dismissed it as quickly as it had come.

She got home, fed and checked all the horses, and headed toward the vet's.

When she arrived, she parked out front, and the tech let her into the clinic. The blunt, rusty-sweet odor of iodine wrinkled Ivy's nose before she entered the exam bay. In the central stanchion, Dr. Clark was running a plastic tube into a horse's nose. Ivy smacked her lips as her mouth suddenly tasted of garlic. Can't get away from DMSO at the vet clinic. *Blech.*

A fresh red and purple bruise swelled on the doctor's cheek, and the perfect impression of a horse's incisors, exquisitely outlined in red, marked his left arm.

"What does the other guy look like?"

"Like a black and white mare with strangles."

"What? My horse did that to you?" Ivy cringed. Had she made the worst mistake of her rescue career with that mare?

He picked up a large stainless-steel syringe and put the end into the tube. When he pressed on the plunger, the horse shook its head and tried to back up, but the metal pipe walls left it no room to maneuver. It raised its head and pawed, but the vet moved with it, forcing the rest of the medication into the tube. He listened to the horse's belly with a stethoscope, then carefully withdrew the tube.

He stripped off his exam gloves. "Your mare does not like men. She hasn't given Dr. Mueller any trouble, or any of the techs. Except for Michael. Anyway, I've put her on penicillin and streptomycin—if we don't get this cleared up before she foals, the baby's almost certain to get it, too. We don't want to go there if we can help it."

Ivy ran a hand through her long hair. Maybe I should have listened to Julie and picked the other two healthy horses. But I couldn't leave her. "Sorry about that. She's obviously been abused...So, you think the baby's nine months? Is there enough time for the antibiotics to work?"

"There should be. But it can be dicey when pregnant mares are under a lot of stress. Hopefully, the groceries and the treatment will keep her from aborting."

Or having a premature foal, because where is the money going to come from for that? Ivy sighed. "I'd like to come out and see her."

"Sure, sure. You know where she is. Just make sure you put shoe covers on while you're out there."

The black and white mare stood in the far corner of the double-sized stall, pulling hay from a manger and chewing. She looked up as Ivy approached, unafraid, but aware, unvarnished skepticism on her face. Ivy didn't enter the stall. Partly because she wanted to minimize contact with the nasty bug the mare was sure to be shedding, and partly because if the mare decided to charge her, there was no one in the barn to pull her out of the way of angry hooves and gnashing teeth.

"Hey, pretty girl. We need to find you a name—Tag 478 doesn't suit you."

The mare flicked an ear and jerked another bite of hay from the rack. Her eyes never left Ivy.

"How about Domino? Too common. Pie, short for piebald? No, don't want to combine horses and food items." Ivy gnawed the inside of her cheek. "But what about Velvet? When you gain some weight, you'll be very elegant."

The horse snorted a big blob of snot onto the floor.

Ivy swayed under the hot water in her shower. If she leaned against the wall, she might fall asleep—she was tired to the bone. When she had gotten home, she found that one of her dogs had broken through a window to go after a skunk. She taped a trash bag over the gaping frame and made a pharmacy run for large quantities of hydrogen peroxide and baking soda. Dish soap, she had. Yay, Costco.

Luckily, Eddie had opted to stay in the house and leave the skunk-chasing to his buddy. It took three rounds of dousing Twilight with peroxide, scrubbing with baking soda and detergent, then rinsing before the hairy German Shepherd mix was mostly stink-free. It might take her two days to dry, though it seemed like half of her hair had ended up on Ivy. She couldn't show up at work tomorrow looking like a werewolf, so into the shower she went for the second time that evening.

She tried to keep herself awake by thinking about what $10,000 could do for her rescue. Stock up on hay. Pay off the vet bills she never seemed to be able to get on top of. Buy new tires for the trailer.

Her mother had left her the property when she died, so she didn't have rent or a mortgage. That helped a lot. Last year, she'd started going to night school on Tuesdays, Thursdays, and Saturdays to finish off her bachelor's degree. Her company would reimburse her when she graduated with an 'A' or 'B' average, and she'd move up two pay grades. She knew it would be worth it in the long run, but right now, it was a killer. She just had to hold on until spring—seven long months until May—but at least she could see the light at the end of the tunnel.

Ivy shut off the water, wrung out her hair, and reached for a towel.

Knowing that she'd fall asleep if she kept sitting in her office chair, Ivy had to go for a walk at lunch time. It felt good to get her blood flowing and breathe in some fresh air. The sweltering summer heat had just started to break, and it was not unpleasant outside, as long as she stayed on the shady part of the sidewalk.

Her phone rang.

"Hello?"

"Yes. Is this Miss Stonewall?"

"Who wants to know?"

"This is Helen Butterfield. I'm on the Organizing Committee for the Salt River Group kickoff gala. I have you listed as the representative for Copper Penny Horse Rescue. I wanted to personally invite you to the first planning meeting this Saturday at 3:00 at the Bennington Hotel."

"Oh! Thank you. But I can't be there right at three—I have class until then. I could probably be there by 3:30 or so—would that be alright?" Her excitement at being on the high level committee was tempered by the number of responsibilities she already had.

"Of course! Come as soon as you can. We'll see you then."

She ended the call before Ivy could respond.

Traffic was worse than Ivy expected. She couldn't see around the blue whale-sized suburban ahead, and the thumping bass of the car next to her rattled her innards unpleasantly. She was never so grateful for a freeway exit in her life.

Ivy had packed a protein bar in her purse, because she knew she wouldn't have time to stop and grab something between class and driving to the gala meeting. She tore open the wrapper as she waited at a stoplight. *Julie, why, why, why did you have to be out of town during the gala? I don't have time for this.*

She was parked and inside the conference room by 3:25. *Not bad.* Ivy hid her hands in the pockets of the hoodie she'd brought in case the hotel had the AC set to 'arctic.' In her jeans and cotton sweater, she felt underdressed in the opulent lobby. She found the conference room and slipped into a chair in the back row. A few people turned around to look at her, but she ignored them.

A woman was at the front of the ballroom, speaking from behind a podium, and Ivy thought it was likely to be Helen Butterfield, but she didn't really know.

"Again," Probably Helen said, "I want to thank you for coming and helping to support this fundraiser that is helping to support you. When you signed in, you should have picked up your packet, which will have the information about what committee you're on and where it will meet for the breakout session. Please take a fifteen-minute break and reconvene accordingly."

Ivy looked at her packet. She was on the Welcoming Committee, which would meet in the Jade Room. She stifled a yawn and decided to get a cup of coffee from the bar on the way over. Julie usually looked after the horses on Saturdays, but she had left for a business trip on Thursday and wouldn't be back for a week. Ivy had gotten up at 5:30 to take care of the horses before her first class at 8:00, and the four hours of sleep she'd had last night was catching up to her.

She asked her phone to remind her to go to the Jade Room in ten minutes. As she sipped her coffee, she used an app to order some books she needed for class. She plugged her device into a lipstick charger and wished she could recharge her own batteries just as easily. The alarm sounded, and she chugged the rest of her coffee before heading to the conference room.

The Jade Room was much smaller than the main ballroom, and of course, painted green, with remarkably well done trompe l'oeil Asian-themed sculptures on the walls. Dragons, cherry trees, and fu dogs seemed to be in their own recessed display alcoves, but Ivy had to touch them to realize they were just clever paint jobs. Still, it was far larger than necessary. Eight folding chairs were arranged in a semi-circle, with one at the front center. Five people had already taken their seats. They smiled at her when she sat down. She smiled back. Ivy's jaw dropped when she saw who sat down in the center chair.

He grinned at her. "Hello, Ivy." His eyes scanned the rest of the committee. "Let's start by introducing ourselves and a very short description of our charities. My name is Jax Carter, and my charity is BookStar. We sponsor book donations to school libraries in need of books and fund literacy efforts for people of all ages."

The tall woman at the opposite end of the row from Ivy stood up. "I'm Katherine Edgemont. My charity is Lovin' Bowlfuls, and we're kind of like Meals on Wheels for pets—we take food to people who are shut-ins, or struggling to feed their pets. We also transport the animals to and from the spay and neuter clinic for surgeries and vaccinations."

She sat down, and the next woman remained seated. "I'm Hillary Feinstein, from Story Buddies. We read to children in hospitals and donate books and toys to them."

"I'm Meghan Mondolvo. Green the Greens. We acquire and plant native trees and shrubs in public spaces."

"Ashley Smith. Doggone Safety. We raise money for police K9 equipment, like bullet-proof vests, and also help sponsor them once they retire."

"Hello. My name is Christie Simms. My charity is Horses for Healing, and we sponsor kids to participate in therapeutic horse-riding programs."

Everybody deserves the $10,000. I wish there were more than ten winners. "I'm Ivy Stonewall, Copper Penny Horse Rescue. We save horses. And other animals. But mostly horses."

The meeting went better than most committee meetings that Ivy had been to. Perhaps because the non-profits were used to getting more done with fewer resources than many in Corporate America. On the way out, she paused for a drink of water from one of the carafes at the back of the room.

Jax caught up to her. "I think that was a very productive meeting. We seem to have a good team going here. I really liked your idea about the badges for gala attendees. Maybe to save time at the next meeting, we could hash out the details beforehand."

"Another meeting?"

"Well, I was thinking informally. Over coffee, or maybe dinner?"

Is this actual committee business, or is he asking me on a date? "Let me check my calendar, but I don't think I can do it before Friday." She pulled out her phone.

"Friday is fine. Do you like Thai food?"

"Sure." She scrolled through her calendar.

"Then why don't we meet at Fire Sticks on Bellaire and Chimney Rock at seven?"

"How about 7:30, so I have time to take a shower after I've fed the horses and run the manure spreader?"

He smiled again. "That works for me."

Ivy punched it into her calendar. "Great. See you then."

The shot-gunning of coffee had its consequences. She had to make a pit stop at the ladies' room. When she went to the sink to wash her hands, she saw a big chocolate smear along the top of her lip from the protein bar she'd wolfed down in the car. No wonder everybody had been grinning at her. *And now, for my next feat of grace and skill...*

She wiped her face and headed to her car. She couldn't help feeling a twinge of disappointment. The meeting with Jax must really be about the badges, because who would ask some fool on a date who couldn't even get food in her mouth without missing?

Chapter
Four

JAX WATCHED IVY walk down the hallway. If he were the sort that believed in the power of coincidences, he might think it was fate that kept their paths crossing. But fate had a reputation for being fickle. He tried to analyze why he found Miss Stonewall attractive. In fact, he analyzed everything, and whether that was a character flaw or a life skill was debatable. She was pleasant to look at, without being artificially pretty. He would in no way describe her as 'matronly,' and yet she came across as a nurturer. She'd come up with some good ideas at the meeting, so she was both smart and resourceful. But the biggest thing, he decided, was that she was genuine. She didn't seem to need to play games—just cut to the chase. He liked that in a person. Not just liked. Needed. He couldn't stand people who brought a lot of drama.

This committee had provided the perfect cover for asking her out. If they seemed to click, it was a date. If not, it was just business.

It was Tuesday morning, and Jax shifted in his seat. This week would be a busy one. There was an international trade summit in town, starting tomorrow, although attendees had been arriving since Sunday. So had throngs of protesters, and the scourge of all events, the Black Bloc anarchists, who clung to public gatherings like disease-ridden parasites.

The most recent similar event in Europe had ended with cars being set on fire and bottles and rocks thrown at police.

It had taken three rounds of tear gas and a water cannon to disperse the protesters.

The chief in Houston did not want that mess in his town, where protesters were typically better behaved than in other large cities. Undercover officers had been mobilized weeks before to gather intel about any planned violence. Uniformed officers in riot gear and mounted patrol would be out in force. It would be a long week. Fortunately, the delegates would be clearing out on Friday, and he'd have a rare weekend off.

Jax let his mind wander to the possibility of not waking up alone on Saturday morning, but he quickly dismissed it. No point in setting unreasonable expectations. Still, it had been a while. He shook himself to get his head back in the game. There would be time to think about that after, when there weren't potential bottle-throwing rioters surrounding him.

Roll call was dismissed. He grabbed his gear and stowed it in the trailer.

The protesters had gotten a little rowdy on Thursday night, but with the Black Blockers mostly controlled, there was little enthusiasm for random destruction. Most of them had been neutralized, either through arrest (many of them had warrants) or law enforcement presence. Friday should have been a walk in the park.

At two in the afternoon, some members of a neo-Nazi group started throwing rocks at the Mexican delegation's motorcade. They bounced harmlessly off the bullet-proof glass, and the heavily armored police moved in to shut them down. Officers on horseback hemmed in the rock-throwers. Jax was hyper vigilant—all the skinheads had rifles slung over their backs, and many of them had AR-15s.

The mayor had banned open carry of weapons at protests, in the interest of public safety, but the governor had gotten an eleventh-hour injunction on enforcement of the order.

Jax rubbed his knuckles along his horse's neck. "Hang in there, Ruby."

Above the stink of large numbers of sweaty people, adrenaline, and horse sweat, Jax noticed a sharp, oily smell.

Lighter fluid.

He whipped his head around and saw sunlight glint off glass.

"Fire at ten o'clock!" he shouted.

A figure in a black hoodie with a skull-print bandana tied around his face lit a rag that hung out of a glass bottle.

He hurled the Molotov straight at Jax.

Ruby flinched as it glanced off her face shield and hit the ground, shattering under the feet of the officers. Jax noted the man's bright red running shoes as he fled. Flaming liquid flowed around the feet of both police and protesters, catching some of them alight.

The panicked crowd swept the bomber along with it as people ran blindly away from the spreading fire. Jax spotted him running toward Discovery Green. He couldn't be allowed to get into the underground parking garage—too many levels and too many places to hide. Besides, he might have a car waiting for him there. If not, he'd have plenty of opportunities to steal one. Jax urged Ruby into a trot. Fear-blind or not, nobody was dumb enough to stand in the way of three quarters of a ton of horse coming at them. He couldn't call for backup as all the other officers were, quite literally, putting out fires.

As space opened up, he eased Ruby into a canter. The man in the hoodie ducked down an alley, but Jax gambled that he knew where the man was going and took a shortcut.

People streamed out of the alley, moving slower now. But he couldn't find the man in the hoodie. Had he guessed wrong?

And there they were. The red shoes. The man had taken off the hoodie and bandana to try to blend in with the crowd. As soon as he saw Jax coming for him, he tried elbowing his way through the throng. Some people elbowed back, and one man back-fisted him hard enough to give him a nosebleed. He staggered, then tried to run across the open lawn of the park.

Jax kicked Ruby into a gallop. She would easily run the fleeing man down. She had already made up half the distance between them.

He was vaguely aware that people had stopped to watch the takedown. And then, without warning, a woman with ear-buds in her ears, playing with her phone, wheeled her dou-ble-length stroller with two toddlers in it right into Ruby's path. A modern art installation loomed on the other side, giv-ing Jax no room to swerve.

He had a fraction of a second to decide between bad and worse options.

Ruby took the decision out of his hands. Without break-ing stride, she sailed over the stroller and extended her gal-lop. It only took seconds for her to catch the running suspect, and Jax had to rein her in hard so they didn't overshoot him altogether.

"Red shoes! Stop!"

The man did not stop and veered toward the pond.

"Get him, Ruby."

Before Ruby had become a police horse, she had been a cutting horse. She could deftly separate any steer out of its herd, but she was too tall to beat the speeds of the shorter, lower center-of-gravity horses in competitions, so she'd been donated to the mounted patrol. Humans were not nearly as fast as steers.

Everywhere the man turned, the chestnut mare was already in front of him. After a minute or two, he gave up, raising his hands in the air, and sinking to his knees in the grass.

"Lay down, arms out to the side!"

"By doze!"

"Do it!"

The man whimpered, but complied. Without anonymity and a weapon, the bravado had evaporated like morning dew.

"Cross your feet."

Jax slid off Ruby and handcuffed the Black Blocker. Then he radioed for an ambulance.

People who had stopped to watch started clapping and cheering. And, of course, every single one of them wanted to come up and pet Ruby. He had a tough time keeping his suspect from getting trampled before EMS arrived.

A television crew wasn't far behind. The last thing Jax wanted to do was deal with reporters. What he wanted more than anything was to get back to his team and see if everyone was okay. He wanted to load Ruby up and take her back to the stables for a bath and peppermints for being the superstar that she was. He wanted to take a shower and go meet Ivy.

Instead, what he had was a bloody suspect in custody, a news camera in his face, and a mountain of paperwork in store for him later. And that's if the paramedics didn't transport his prisoner to Ben Taub, the county hospital. That could easily add another twelve hours or more to his day.

"I'm sorry, I can't comment on an ongoing investigation." That got the reporter off his back, but only because people in the crowd were climbing all over each other for the chance to be on TV.

"You should have seen it!"

"It was amazing!"

"Just like a movie!"

"He was so reckless! Almost mowed down a stroller with babies in it! They should sue the city."

"Ruby for president!"

Jax used his laptop to work on his report while the Fire Department paramedics examined the Black Blocker. The EMTs packed his prisoner's nose with gauze—it wasn't broken—and left.

Fortunately, no one had been seriously injured when the protests turned violent. There were some scrapes and bruises, and a few minor burns, but no one was transported to a hospital. The neo-Nazis that had tried to start the riot were in custody. Based on the tattoos many of them sported, it wasn't their first time behind bars. A patrol unit arrived to valet park Jax's suspect at the HPD Hilton.

He looked at his watch. It was only 3:30. There was a chance he could still make his date. He held off texting Ivy to cancel, just in case.

He shouldn't have waited. It was almost 7:00 before the horses were loaded up and he had a chance to text Ivy.

"I am so sorry. Got stuck at work. Could we reschedule? Please?"

She hadn't replied by the time they got back to the stables. Probably driving to the restaurant. He felt bad about the cancellation and the short notice, but it couldn't be helped. His schedule could be unpredictable. If she couldn't be flexible, then there probably wasn't any point in dating her. Of course, she had no idea what his job was, so how could she know he wasn't just blowing her off for a better offer? Right now, it was out of his hands. Things would either work out or they wouldn't.

Ruby was the second from last on the trailer, so she was the second one to come off. He went straight to the wash rack and gave her a bath, scrubbing away all the grime and saddle marks. He used a sweat scraper to squeegee off the excess water, then led her to her stall. Her dinner was already waiting for her, and she flicked her ears as she buried her nose in the bucket of pellets.

Jax cleaned and put away his gear, adding his saddle pad to the laundry pile. He'd gotten his report done so that the patrol could transport his prisoner, but because the prisoner had been injured, he had to fill out additional forms and make sure his body camera video was uploaded and tagged.

He woke his cell phone. 10:07 and sighed. There was a text message that had come in while he was tending to Ruby.

Ivy wasn't available over the weekend.

At least Flip would be happy to see him when he got home.

Chapter
Five

IVY HEARD HER text chime go off. Whoever it was, they would have to wait. She was trying to merge into the one moving lane on the Beltway to get around the jack-knifed eighteen-wheeler that sprawled across the other three lanes. Normally, she would just use her phone's voice assistant to reply, but she needed every ounce of concentration she could muster.

She was going to be late. Chimney Rock and Bellaire was still another twenty minutes away. Without traffic. At this rate, it would be twenty minutes before she was able to merge into the lane that crawled like a drunken snail down the tollway, bending this way and that to avoid the debris field from the accident.

Ivy drummed her fingers on the steering wheel in frustration. Traffic was part of life in America's fourth largest city. If Jax couldn't be flexible about traffic, there may not be a good reason to go any further with him.

In the end, it was 7:45 when she arrived at Fire Sticks. Fifteen minutes late wasn't so bad, was it? She rooted through her bag to find her phone.

There was a text from Jax.

He wasn't coming. Seriously? After she'd sat in traffic for almost an hour? Ivy glowered out the car window. A couple walked past her car. The woman, wearing a clingy red dress, tossed her hair and laughed. The man couldn't keep his hands off of her. It made the sting of Jax's ditching her more acute.

Fresh blood trickled from old wounds. Wonder what her name is?

Don't jump to conclusions. Just because Chance ran around like a cat in heat doesn't mean all men are like that. At least he messaged you. He could have just ghosted.

Ivy didn't entirely believe her own pep talk. She didn't even know what he did for a living. Who knows? Maybe he really was stuck at work. Deciding to give him the benefit of the doubt, she returned his text.

"Weekend's booked. Maybe Sunday. Will let you know. But probably not."

She was at the restaurant, and she was starving, so she might as well go in and eat.

The waiter led her to a table. White linen tablecloths. Could be expensive.

Ivy ordered iced tea and looked at the menu. The prices weren't as bad as she'd feared. She'd planned on paying for her own meal anyway, but now that it was just her, eating out seemed extravagant. But she couldn't bear to go sit in that traffic again, and besides, she'd already ordered tea.

To appease her inner comptroller, she ordered vegetable fried rice, the cheapest thing on the menu. As the waiter hurried off, she glanced up at the big-screen TV at the end of the room. Her horse-dar went off—there was Houston's mounted patrol splashed across the news. Something about trouble at a protest downtown.

There was a brief clip of a mounted officer arresting some guy in fluorescent red running shoes, then the video cut to a close-up of the officer.

"I'm sorry, I can't comment on an ongoing investigation." The closed captions flicked onto the screen.

Ivy set her tea down hard, too close to the edge of the table. Tea soaked the carpet. Ice got in her shoe.

But she just stared at Jax on the big screen. A moment later, he was gone, and the reporter was getting 'man on the street' commentary from bystanders.

The busboy rushed over with towels and a sweeper.

"I am so sorry for making such a mess. Can I help clean up?"

"No! You sit. Happens all the time."

Ivy cringed and then moved over a seat. She'd just have to add extra to the tip.

While she waited for her food, she scanned the local news outlets on her phone, looking for more information about the protest disturbance. She found several takes on it, and while Jax wasn't mentioned by name, there were several stills of him, on and off a gorgeous red mare.

On the one hand, Ivy was happy that she had proof that Jax really was working late. That eased her mind, and the fact he worked with horses as his day job didn't hurt a thing. She frowned. Maybe it helped too much? Would a mutual love of horses cloud her judgement? Still, she'd seen him scratching under the red mare's mane as she stood beside him, how she lowered her head and stretched her neck contentedly. Thoughts of those warm, strong hands on her own body made her shiver.

Ivy was both disappointed and grateful when the waiter set her plate on the table.

Ivy sighed. How had she ended up in the dark with Jax? She couldn't remember. Warm breath caressed her cheek. Was he growing a beard? Short whiskers tickled her lips and chin. Too dark to see, she had to imagine the square line of his jaw, his green eyes with the little brown flecks that sparkled like gold in the right light. Then a kiss, gentle and warm. And wet. This guy was a little weird. The slobbering was not at all sexy. She opened her eyes and found herself looking straight into two large black nostrils.

"Aaah!" Ivy jerked away and wiped her mouth.

Twilight barked and wagged her tail.

Ivy blinked a few times, trying to orient herself. She was on the couch, her corporate finance textbook in her lap. Must have fallen asleep doing her homework. Twilight had apparently been none too pleased about breakfast being late on a Sunday morning and had taken steps to remedy the situation.

"Okay, okay. I'm up." Ivy marked her place and closed the book before she stretched and stood up. She had a crick in her neck from sleeping at a weird angle.

After all the animals were fed, she sat down to her own breakfast of coffee and cold cereal. She looked around the kitchen as she chewed. She'd need to add a tidy-up to her list of chores. The farmhouse sink she'd had installed was great for scrubbing horse equipment, and the occasional injured wild animal, but it also tended to collect an unhelpful number of dirty dishes. Crumbs around the toaster stood out on the white Formica.

Thunder grumbled outside. Sullen clouds obscured the early morning sun. The breeze had been a nice change from yesterday's warm, still air. The weather forecast predicted rain and thunderstorms for today and tomorrow.

Instead of working on the fence like she'd planned, she would be inside doing her homework. If there was a break in the storms, she might even see if Jax was available for lunch. She smiled at the thought, then inwardly cringed at the memory of her morning wake-up. Why did her mind even go there? At least she and Twilight were the only ones who knew about it, and Twilight wasn't telling anyone.

It was just after ten when she finished her paper on "Marketing Strategies for the Twenty-First Century." She needed a break.

Now would be the perfect time to text Jax. She picked up her phone. And put it back down. A snack first. She'd been burning up the glucose with all that intensive brain work she'd been doing, right?

Ivy ate an apple and a protein bar, then washed her hands, scrubbing at her nails to make sure there weren't any traces of dirt, real or imagined, lodged there from her morning's horse care activities. She picked up the phone again, then looked out the window to check the weather. It was barely drizzling.

No big deal. It was just lunch. To talk about the charity gala. And he might not even be available. She tapped the messaging icon on her phone and found his thread. "Lunch?" No, too abrupt. She erased it. "Just wondering if you might be able to meet for lunch." No, that's not right, either. She erased that. "You free for lunch?" Was that the right amount of casual? She'd find out soon. Ivy sent the message.

Jax responded almost immediately. "Sure. Where?"

She got up and got a drink of water. Then she looked out the window again, just in case the weather had changed in the last five minutes. Stop being ridiculous. You aren't in middle school—you're an adult scheduling a lunch meeting about an ongoing project. Pick a spot and send the text already!

"How about Rigatoni on I10 and Voss? 1:00."

"See you then."

Ivy had just stepped out of the shower when her phone rang. She'd left it on the vanity so she could hear it, just in case. She blotted off her hand and stood dripping on the bathmat.

"Ivy? It's Dr. Mueller. Your mare is going into labor. She bagged up tight last night, and she started leaking milk this morning. Her water hasn't broken, but she's showing all the signs. I'm a bit worried about her because she's not in such good shape."

"Okay. I'm on my way."

She dried off and got dressed. Maybe this Jax thing just isn't meant to be. A needle of regret pierced her heart. He seemed so right for her. Too good to be true....

Ivy picked up the phone and called him.

"Ivy?"

"I'm really sorry, but it's my turn to cancel."

"What's up?"

"My rescue mare that's at the vet's? She just went into labor. The baby may be a preemie. We don't know how far along she is, but the vet thinks maybe nine months. I'm leaving now, and I'll probably be there the rest of the afternoon."

"Oh. Well...emergencies happen. I hope your mare's okay."

"Thanks. I was really looking forward to meeting up with you. Guess I'll see you at the next meeting."

"Be careful on the slick roads. See you soon."

Ivy's disappointment was quickly displaced by anxiety about Velvet and her foal. Would Velvet be able to take care of her baby? Would the foaling set back all of her progress? Was the foal even developed enough to survive?

She tried to force worry out of her head by turning up the car radio. However, the DJ seemed to be playing every sad song in the station's stash. After fifteen minutes, she turned it off. The silence was no better. At the next stoplight, she connected her phone and started up a podcast. It helped some— at least her hands weren't trembling when she arrived at the equine hospital.

Mary sat behind the front desk.

"Hey, Ivy." She gestured to the big-screen TV on the wall to Ivy's right. "We've got Velvet on MareCam."

On the screen, Velvet stood miserably in her stall, lifting and flicking her bandaged tail, then shifting her weight. The grain in her feeder sat untouched.

"How long has she been like this?"

"Dr. Mueller called as soon as she started squirting milk."

It's only been about an hour. Calm down. "I'm sorry. I wasn't trying to imply that you weren't taking care of her."

Mary nodded. "I know. Make yourself comfortable. You know if that mare even suspects that you're watching her, she won't drop her foal."

Ivy half-laughed. She turned the waiting room chair around to face the small table littered with brochures. "I brought my homework to do while I wait. Statistics class."

"You just make yourself at home, sugar."

"You know I will."

She glanced up at the screen between problems. Velvet had quieted and appeared to be taking a nap. The rain had picked up, and lightning flickered in the distance, too far away for thunder to catch up to it. Maybe Velvet was waiting for the storm to pass.

Ivy closed her statistics book. Done! She'd only been there forty-five minutes, but it felt like hours. If she could just find that Frida Kahlo book in her backpack, she'd be able to finish up her essay on "Pièce de résistance: Art and the Drivers of Social Change."

The cowbell on the front door clattered.

Mary stood up. "Jax? What on earth brings you out in this weather?"

Ivy smelled something warm and cheesy before she turned to see him, water running off his yellow rain slicker, wiping his feet on the mat at the front door. He was carrying three pizza boxes. He leaned his head back, and the hood fell off, revealing his tousled sandy hair and day-old stubble.

"What are you doing here?" Ivy asked, too surprised not to repeat Mary's question.

"I knew you didn't have any lunch, and Dr. Mueller and her staff would probably be here late with your horse, so here I am." He grinned at Mary. "I know you and Dr. Mueller like pineapple and jalepeño." He set the top box on Mary's desk. He turned to Ivy. "But I didn't know what you liked, so I got plain cheese. One cheese for the techs, too." He set a second box on top of the first.

Ivy blinked and swallowed. "I-I don't know what to say. You drove all the way out here in the rain with pizza. That's...."

Mary took two boxes and disappeared into the back of the clinic.

"Our get-together seems to be struggling to happen on its own, so I thought I'd help it out. Sorry, it's not Rigatoni's, but it would have been cold by the time I got here. Hector's down the street isn't too bad, though."

Jax set the last box of pizza down on the counter and shrugged off his raincoat. He draped it over the back of a chair to dry. "You hungry?"

"Starved."

Ivy moved her papers out of the way, and Jax brought the pizza box over and set it down on the table. They each took a slice.

"That's Velvet up there." Ivy pointed to the TV. "The black and white one."

On the screen, Velvet took up one quarter of the view, while another pregnant mare snoozed in the opposite corner. The other two frames were dark. Velvet was sweating, standing with her nose almost to the straw. She lay down. She stood back up. The mare walked in a circle and lay back down, flat on her side. Her ribs heaved up and down. She stood back up.

Jax nodded at the display. "She's getting ready. Shouldn't be too much longer now."

Something grey protruded from under her tail, and what looked like gallons of liquid spewed out, drenching Velvet's hind legs and the stall.

Mary paged Dr. Mueller over the intercom.

Ivy startled. She hadn't heard her return.

The vet replied. "Let's give her ten minutes, then Kelly and I will go down there. Ivy and Jax can come, too. Hey, thanks for the pizza. Not all heroes wear capes."

Velvet was still in the quarantine barn, and rain was still bucketing down. They piled into Dr. Mueller's truck and drove down to the stable. She backed into the wide aisleway, and they clambered out, sheltered from the rain.

Dr. Mueller and Kelly approached Velvet's stall quietly. Ivy and Jax hung back, peering through the stall bars at the corner where Velvet couldn't see them. She was flat on her side now, her quarters toward Ivy.

The vet crouched by Velvet's head and stroked her face. "Easy, girl. We're here to help."

She reached down to Velvet's jaw to take her pulse. The doctor moved to the mare's hind quarters and pulled her tail back. Ivy could see two feet and a nose. Baby's in the right position. So far, so good.

Velvet groaned as she pushed. The foal's shoulders cleared the birth canal, and it came slithering out in a mess of membranes and liquid. Dr. Mueller made sure the baby's nose was clear and did a cursory examination.

"It's a boy."

He was completely black, and smaller than Ivy would have expected from a big draft mare. The foal raised his head. His ears were perfectly upright, not the bent, floppy ears of a preemie. Had Dr. Mueller been wrong about his age? Maybe because he was so little...

Velvet was still lying flat on her side. She hadn't even tried to look at her baby. Ivy wanted to rush into the stall and do something, anything to get the mare to move.

Dr. Mueller checked Velvet's pulse again, then looked at her gums. "Kelly, get the ultrasound, and bring a bucket."

The tech hurried toward the truck.

The doctor stood up and came over to where Ivy and Jax stood. Ivy could tell from the look on her face that whatever she had to say, it wasn't going to be good.

"I think she's got a bleed. She's looking shocky, but it could also be that she used up all the energy she had pushing out this foal. I'm going to do an ultrasound and see if I can find anything."

Ivy suddenly felt cold. She didn't say anything, because she was afraid she'd cry. It took some moments to notice her shoulder felt warm, the icy knot being soothed away by a gentle, rhythmic stroking. She turned her head to see Jax rubbing her shoulder. She both craved the warmth of his touch and resented the intrusion of a virtual stranger. Had she foolishly wasted the rescue's money on a lost cause, potentially letting perfectly healthy horses go to slaughter?

She started to shiver. Jax put his arm loosely around her. Ivy stiffened, then relaxed as she watched the vet and tech set up the portable ultrasound machine. After they were done wanding the mare, Kelly broke it down and took it away. She came back with a stable sheet and covered Velvet with it.

Dr. Mueller approached Ivy. "I'm afraid she has a uterine arterial bleed. Right now, it's bleeding into the broad ligament that supports the uterus. That's good—there's no place for the blood to go, so it applies its own pressure to the hemorrhage, stopping the bleeding. But you have to know, there's a fifty percent mortality rate in these cases. Given her condition, I don't think her odds are quite that good. I'm going to run some fluids on her to keep her blood volume stable. I'll also give her some Banamine and put her on naloxone. Kelly and I will get the drip going. What I need you to do is collect as much of her colostrum as you can and see if you can get the foal to drink it. Kelly will bring you a bottle once we get the IV established."

She handed Ivy the bucket and turned back to her patient.

Ivy looked at Jax. "Have you ever milked a mare before?"

"No. You?"

"Only once, and she was standing up."

There was no way that they'd be able to use a bucket to collect the precious, antibody-laden first milk when Velvet was lying down. Kelly found them a styro coffee cup, and they turned it on its side, collected a few squirts, then dumped the contents into the bucket. Kelly dried the baby with a towel while they worked. He raised his head and whickered to his mother. Fuzzy foal mane stuck out in all directions, making him look like an equine Albert Einstein.

Thunder boomed above them, rattling the barn doors. The lights flickered and went out. The emergency lights above the far door came on, but that didn't help much on the dairying front. Jax pulled out his cell phone and used it as a flashlight.

They were still milking when the colt shakily struggled to his feet and let out a high-pitched whinny. Velvet raised her head and nickered to him. She tried to roll onto her sternum so she could stand up but abandoned the effort and laid back down flat. The foal staggered around, unable to control his long, knobby legs. Jax took the bucket and retreated from the stall. He poured its contents into the foal-sized baby bottle that Kelly had given them and handed it to Ivy.

She hummed All the Pretty Little Horses as she approached the foal. He tried to run but was too uncoordinated. Once she brought the nipple to his muzzle, though, he knew exactly what to do. He guzzled from the bottle, head-butting it and nearly knocking it out of Ivy's hands. He'd drunk all there was, and he wanted more.

"That's a good sign," said Dr. Mueller. "Kelly, can you mix up some FoaLac?"

"Sure thing." Using her own phone as a light, she took the bottle and disappeared down the dark aisle.

The vet rubbed the foal's neck. "He's small, but I think he's full term. His lungs sounded good when I listened earlier."

Jax ran his hand along fuzzy mane atop the baby's neck. "He needs a name."

"I'll let you guys work on that." Dr. Mueller shuffled back towards Velvet, and Jax lit the way for her. "Looks like she's still got some colostrum—you might want to see if you can get the rest."

Kelly came back with the bottle of milk and kept the foal occupied while Ivy and Jax finished milking Velvet.

Now that his belly was full, the foal awkwardly lay down next to his mother for a snooze. Velvet nickered to him, but she was still too weak to get up.

Ivy stroked the mare's side. I know you don't know me very well, and I'm so sorry for how you were treated before. Please stay with us, Velvet. That little guy over there really needs you.

"I have to get back to the farm and feed the horses. I would ask Julie, but she's out of town, so it's just me." Ivy stood up.

"We'll monitor her and feed the little guy. If she makes it through the night, there's a good chance she'll survive. I'll call you in the morning."

"Thanks, Dr. Mueller. I appreciate all that you're doing."

The vet nodded. "You be careful driving home. I'll run you back up to the clinic. Still have some treatments I have to do before I come back out here."

In the front office, Mary had lit some scented candles for light. Vanilla, Ginger Melon, Sea Breeze, and Sandalwood were never intended to be burned together. Ivy coughed.

Jax started putting on his rain slicker.

"I still can't get over how you drove out here with pizza for everybody, then helped out with Velvet. You're like...a knight in Kevlar armor, swooping in on a big chestnut mare."

He stopped and cocked his head, the candlelight casting shadows under his cheekbones.

"I saw you on the news Friday."

"Ah." A bemused grin took over his mouth. "Well, we never actually got a chance to finish our pizza."

Ivy raised an eyebrow. Is he angling for something? "Why don't you bring it with you and come help me feed the horses? I'll get done twice as fast, and then we'll have plenty of time to...finish the pizza."

That didn't quite come out the way I intended. I hope he doesn't get the wrong idea. Or maybe I do. Stop thinking, Ivy. You're not helping.

She borrowed a Post-It note from Mary and wrote her address on it. "Just in case you lose me in the rain."

"Let's go feed some horses."

Chapter
Six

THE RAIN HAD eased from torrential to merely heavy. Wipers on high just kept the windshield clear enough to see Ivy's ice blue Accord ahead. He was glad she wasn't in the car with him. Driving in the rain at night made him anxious. Not panic attack level, but he could feel his heart thudding behind his ribs and his breathing was fast and shallow. It was an old wound, and yet it still tyrannized him, an accident that had gouged an indelible scar across both his heart and his mind.

Jax tried to shake off the fear by focusing on Ivy. He liked the way she sat quietly and talked to the horses when she thought no one was watching. He also liked the way she filled out her clothes—who needs a gym when you're stacking hay and mucking stalls every day? The pretense of getting together to talk about the gala had fallen away. She seemed to want to see him, see Jax, not the Welcoming Committee chairman. Surely that was a good thing.

He made a game of guessing, based on what he knew of her so far, what her place would be like. Probably not too big. She said she had acreage and a lot of horses, and he suspected the barn would be nicer than her house. And, of course, a dog. She'd have at least one dog.

The slow traffic on 290 slowed even more, as ponding water covered one lane and cars tried to merge into the single passable lane. A black pickup got between him and Ivy, and he felt a flash of aggression.

His inner coach shook his head. "Boy, you barely know this girl, and look at you."

The slope of the highway increased slightly, and the water ran off it in sheets. No more flooding, at least for now. Ivy changed back to the right lane, and Jax dropped in behind her. Finally, she exited, and he followed her down a back road that zigged and zagged at right angles. Scattered houses huddled behind fancy entry gates. After a while, she turned down a gravel driveway. An aluminum gate opened, and Ivy drove through.

She parked near a double-wide trailer and got out of her car, a polka dot umbrella sprouting through the door as she opened it. He parked next to her and pulled the hood on his rain slicker up before he joined her in the deluge.

Water splashed around them as he followed her out to the stable, the wind driving the rain almost horizontally. As they approached the closed barn door, a high-pitched chatter came from inside.

Jax put his hand out to stop Ivy. "Sounds like a raccoon. Maybe I should go first."

"It's really okay."

"They can be dangerous."

Ivy shrugged. "Suit yourself."

It was dark in the barn, but as soon as the door opened, horses nickered. Ivy flipped the light switch.

Jax found himself face to face with a three-legged raccoon. It was chattering at them from a hammock inside a large cage in the first stall by the door.

Ivy grinned. "That's Amos. I found him on the road one morning. Hit by a car. His pelvis was broken, and the vet couldn't save one hind leg, but he gets around pretty well, considering." Ivy's brow crinkled. "The rescue does have a permit to keep him."

"I'm sure you do. I'm not the Game Warden." *I'm just the idiot who tried to save you from your own pet raccoon.*

"He likes shiny things, and he's faster than you think, so be careful if you get close to him. He's a notorious pickpocket."

A horse whinnied loudly and pawed the stall door.

"Alright, Silver. Coming."

Jax followed Ivy down the barn aisle. There was room for about twenty horses, but more than half of the stalls stood empty. A breezeway crossed the aisle about midway down. There was a room on each of three corners, and a set of crossties in the fourth. To Jax's left were doors labeled 'Office' and 'Tack Room.' On the right, 'Feed Room.' Ivy unlocked that one and stepped inside.

On the far wall, there was a shelf labeled with horses' names, and buckets with matching labels sat in neat rows.

Ivy gathered the six buckets from one shelf into a stack.

Jax gestured toward the shelves. "What would you like me to do?"

She handed him the buckets. "Start with Mingo, opposite from Amos, and just dump each one in the feeder. Ivy stacked the other row of buckets and started on the raccoon's side of the aisle.

When the grain was distributed, she handed Jax a manure fork. "I apologize in advance. The horses are usually turned out all day, but with the thunderstorms, they've been inside."

Cozy little kitchen.

Jax dried his hands and forearms on the dishtowel and hung it back up, nearly knocking over the potted basil that perched precariously on the narrow window ledge.

"Thank you so much for helping out." There was that crooked smile again.

"My pleasure." He hadn't really minded mucking stalls. He was just grateful not to be sitting home alone. Five years was long enough to be out in the cold.

"Let me at least cook you dinner."

A loud crack of thunder shook the house. The lights flickered but stayed on. One of Ivy's dogs, a solid black one that may or may not have been a shepherd mix, crept out from under the table, tail between her legs, and leaned against Ivy.

"Poor Twilight. Thunder's not going to get you. Don't worry." She stroked the dog's muzzle, then looked up at Jax. "Be right back."

When she returned, she had a spandex dog shirt, which she wrapped snugly around the craven hound. "There you go."

Huge, fluffy white Eddie, Ivy's other dog, sprawled on the floor nearby. He wasn't overtly menacing, but he kept his eye on Jax.

Ivy opened the pantry and moved a few things around. "How about spinach fettuccini with puttanesca sauce? It's either that or ramen noodles. I've got broccoli and peppers in the fridge."

"Sure. Fettuccini's great. What can I do?"

"Nothing. You've already done so much. Sit. Tell me about your charity."

"Bookstar." He leaned back in the chair and stretched his legs out in front of him. Eddie flicked an ear and smacked his lips. Jax sat up straighter and pulled his legs back a little. "I got the idea back when I used to be on a WET."

Ivy filled the pot with water. "What's that?"

"Warrant Execution Team. Anyway, we had to go pick up this guy who shot somebody in the head in a fight over a parking spot. We made the entry, guy was there with a lit crack pipe in the kitchen. A woman was passed out on the floor, had to call EMS for her, and there were two little kids in the living room. The girl was maybe five or six, and the boy was around four."

"Those kids must have been terrified."

"Oh, yeah. They were just screaming, and nobody could calm them down. Can't really blame them—mom's OD'd on the floor, dad's in handcuffs, and there's officers in full tactical gear everywhere."

Ivy popped a loaf of frozen bread in the oven. "How is this related to books?"

"My niece was about the same age as the girl, and her birthday was coming up that weekend. My sister had told me what to get for her, so I had some books and a doll in my squad, so I went out and got them. Gave the doll to the girl and sat and read them Dr. Seuss until CPS could come and pick them up. The kids just seemed so amazed by the whole story thing. I asked what kinds of books their mom read to them, and she said no one ever read to them. I just couldn't imagine parents not reading bedtime stories to their kids, you know? Any intervention I can do now that helps prevent me from having to arrest them later is a good thing."

Ivy's eyes held Jax's as she nodded slowly. "That's very civic-minded. Do you have kids yourself?"

He waited until she finished rinsing the vegetables to reply. "No." He nearly started to explain why but stopped himself. *No* was good enough for now.

"Me either." The chef knife thunked against the cutting board as she sliced the veggies. "Maybe someday."

That's far enough down this road. Jax spotted a hardcover book on the table. *Essentials of Corporate Finance.* "That looks like a real page turner you're reading."

Ivey followed his glance to the textbook. "Night school. Working on my Business Administration degree. I'm an administrative assistant at an engineering company. Once I graduate, my boss said he will move me into a business analyst position, which is a lot more money. If I make all As and Bs, they'll even reimburse my tuition."

"Wow. How much longer to you have to go?"

"I graduate in May. Assuming I don't fail any classes."

"So, you have a full-time job, run a horse rescue, go to night school, and are volunteering for the Salt River Group charity gala. Do you sleep?" *Doesn't seem to be much time for a new man in that schedule.*

Ivy laughed and nearly spilled pasta sauce as she poured it from the jar into the saucepan. "Sometimes. My partner—business partner—Julie, says I'm chronically overcommitted."

"That's a good way of putting it. Are you sure there's nothing I can do to help you?"

"If you insist, you can stir these vegetables."

Jax made his way to the kitchen and Ivy handed him a spoon.

He stood next to her, pushing the food around in the skillet. Broccoli and bell pepper glistened with olive oil as they sizzled in the pan. His stomach growled—that single piece of pizza had been a long time ago.

The storm had mostly blown over, but the hush of gentle rain fell on the roof. The food smelled better by the minute. There was a lot more to Ivy than just a pretty face. Jax knew he'd have to leave before too much longer, but it was the last thing he wanted to do.

"I think those are done."

Jax looked at the pan. The peppers were starting to blacken around the edges, so he turned off the burner.

Ivy drained the pasta. "Everything's ready. Let me get you a plate."

While he was serving himself noodles, she sawed the small loaf of bread in half. They were both hungry and talked little during the meal. After Ivy cleared away the dishes, she rested her hands on the counter. "I forgot I had some wine in the fridge. Would you care for a glass?"

"Wish I could, but I'm going to have to get on the road soon."

"I guess we'll have to talk about the gala another time, then."

"Definitely."

"You've been amazing today." Ivy stood on tiptoe and kissed his cheek.

Jax fought the urge to bend and put his mouth to hers. It was too soon. He knew if he kissed her, he'd want more. That might scare her away. "An amazing afternoon with an amazing lady."

The color rose in her cheeks as she walked him to the door. He reached for his keys in his back pocket. They weren't there. He tried the other back pocket, then the front ones.

"I can't find my keys."

"I bet I know where they are."

Ivy grabbed a flashlight and her umbrella while Jax pulled on his slicker. She shone the light along the path to the stable. There were no keys to be seen. She pulled open the barn door and turned on the light. "Sorry guys." She turned to the raccoon. "Amos, did you steal Jax's keys?"

The raccoon chattered.

Something silver glittered from Amos' water dish.

"Just as I thought." Ivy opened the door to the cage and closed it quickly behind her. Amos turned in his hammock to watch her. She paused to scratch behind his ears and under his chin before she retrieved the keys and exited the cage. "They were completely under water." She held the key fob out to him.

"The remote might still work. Otherwise, I can't deactivate the ignition kill switch."

"Don't try to use it! You can permanently damage it that way. Let's pack it in rice overnight. You're welcome to crash on my couch."

"Sure. Works for me." *Not like I have a choice.*

Back in the kitchen, Ivy got out a mason jar and filled it halfway with white rice. She added Jax's keys and filled it the rest of the way.

"Hopefully that works."

"Guess we'll find out." He had a spare key and remote at home, but that didn't do him any good now.

"Let me get you a blanket." Ivy disappeared through a doorway that Jax reasoned must be her bedroom.

He sat down on the sofa. Not his first choice, if he was going to be spending the night at Ivy's house, but it was for the best. He hadn't exactly been celibate over the last five years, but he hadn't wanted a connection, either. Couldn't do it. Not then. But now? He liked Ivy. Probably more than he should have at this point. If their relationship did turn physical, he wanted it to be more than a sweaty roll in the hay.

Ivy handed him a quilt and a pillow. "I normally get up at five to feed before work. Do you need to be up earlier than that?"

"Just wake me up. I'll help you feed. If the remote isn't working, maybe I can catch a ride into town with you? I can get someone to pick me up and bring me out with the spare key to get my truck."

"Sounds like a plan. There's a bathroom at the end of the hallway. I get a new toothbrush every time I go to the dentist, but I have an electric. If you look in the top drawer of the vanity, there should be a bunch of packaged toothbrushes and sample sizes of toothpaste."

Jax nodded. "Thanks."

"Well. Goodnight then."

"Night."

Ivy closed the door to her bedroom. Eddie curled up in front of it. Jax edged past the dog to the bathroom. When he came back, he covered up with the quilt and lay in the dark, listening to the rain.

Chapter
Seven

WHAT DO YOU mean you slept with him?" Julie almost
shouted over the phone.

"I didn't sleep with him. He spent the night at my house.
On the couch. Amos stole his keys and dumped them in his
water dish so the remote didn't work. Look, Jax's really good
with the horses. And besides, you're the one who keeps telling
me I need to meet a nice guy. Maybe, you'll get a chance to
meet him before the gala."

"You've invited him to the gala?"

"No. He's the chairman of the Welcoming Committee. I'll
be there, working with him."

Julie snorted and teased quietly. "Oh, Ivy. Sleeping your
way to the top."

"Ha. Ha. He's very nice."

"I'm sure. You know I love you to death, and I want
you to be happy. You deserve a better-than-nice guy. I'd like
to meet Jax."

"Yes, Mother."

"I'm someone who cares about you and knows about your
non-stellar track record with men."

"What's that supposed to mean?"

"Two words: Chance Buchanan."

"I can't believe you're throwing that in my face."

"I just don't want you to get hurt. I'll be home Thursday. Why don't you see if he's available for dinner on Friday or Saturday. You can show me how great he is."

"Okay. I will. You'll see."

"When you find out when he's available, text Karen, okay?"

"Sure."

Ivy disconnected.

It had stung at the time she'd said it, but Julie was right about her questionable taste in men. Ivy should have known better than to marry Chance Buchanan. All the red flags were there—she had just chosen to weave them into a decorative scarf to hang around her neck instead of paying attention and getting the hell out.

Chance had big hurt-puppy brown eyes and a sob story that she later found was completely made up. Ivy was the one to bring home all the strays, and there was no doubt that Chance Buchanan was a cur if there ever was one. But he was so sweet.

Until he wasn't.

He'd only hit her the one time, when she'd confronted him about a pair of panties that she'd found in their bed that did *not* belong to her. She'd taken a day off work and filed for divorce the next day. She also had a locksmith change the locks when he went to his part-time at the auto parts store. He'd retaliated by refusing to sign the divorce papers.

What he'd failed to take into account was that most of his things were at Ivy's house—the one her mother had left her before she and Chance had ever met. When she had texted and asked him to meet her for dinner, he'd come prepared with a tale of woe. How much he missed her. How this was their golden opportunity to patch things up.

He had kissed her on the cheek when they met at Buford's BBQ Beef-O-Rama and his breath stank of stale beer.

"Oh, Baby Girl, I miss you so much. I didn't realize you were my heart and soul until you kicked me out."

You probably just forgot that I'm the one with the bigger paycheck. "Really?"

The waiter came for their drink order. Ivy ordered iced tea. Chance ordered a beer.

"I know we can work things out. Let me come home with you and show how much I love you." He waggled his eyebrows in what was apparently meant to be a seductive expression.

No thanks. I know where that thing's been. Ivy reached into her bag and pulled out a pen and the divorce petition. "I need you to sign this."

His eyes welled and crocodile tears trickled down his cheeks. "I'm so sorry. I don't know what I was thinking. I need you, Ivy. I'll be the man you deserve, I swear."

Ivy hesitated. Their relationship hadn't been all bad. When it was good, it was pretty good. Then she rubbed her cheekbone, where his fist had left a bruise. Her mouth was suddenly dry, and her hands damp.

The drinks arrived, and Ivy took a big swallow of tea.

Shaking her head, she again reached into her bag and pulled out a folded piece of paper and a key. "Your stuff is in this storage unit. The first month is paid. If you want the address and the key, you need to sign the papers."

His eyes narrowed and the broken-hearted act dropped like a lead sinker. Ivy forced herself to smile, even though she heard him muttering 'bitch' and worse as he signed his name.

She checked the signature to make sure he hadn't tried to pull a fast one. He hadn't. She took another sip of her tea and tucked the divorce papers into her bag. While she was there, she took three dollars out of her wallet and set them on the table to pay for the tea.

"Goodbye, Chance." Ivy had walked out and never looked back.

Even though she was so much better off without him than with him, the whole process had still been difficult. She didn't know if she could get through another broken relationship, so she kept herself busy, filling every moment with one activity or another. No time to get involved with anyone new.

Ivy took a deep breath and shook herself. The past was a bad neighborhood, and the longer she stayed, the more likely she was to get mugged by a gang of painful memories. She texted Jax, and they decided that the following Wednesday would work for both of them. They could meet Julie and Karen for a late dinner after the gala committee meeting. Ivy texted Karen and let her know the plan.

Normally, the days had wings, but Wednesday was the slowest day on record. She really wanted to see Jax again, and, as much as she hated to admit it, get Julie's and Karen's input. *What if they hated him?*

She was just glad that Julie was feeding the horses this evening so she could make her 6:00 gala planning meeting. The Welcoming Committee was responsible for theme and decorations, music, swag bags, and guest check-in. Ivy wasn't good at any of those things, except for possibly guest check-in.

All during the meeting, Ivy wondered why she was even there. She didn't feel she had anything to add. Much to her relief, Katherine Edgemont had spent hours on Pinterest and had enough decorating ideas for not only this gala, but the next ten as well. Hillary Feinstein's nephew was a professional DJ, and she was sure he'd jump at the chance to work a high-profile event.

And then the hour and a half was up.

"Ladies," Jax said, "I'm out of town next week for work. Why don't you just email the group with any project updates? We've got three weeks until the gala and I think we're in pretty good shape."

Jax and Ivy stayed behind as the other five women filtered out.

He gathered his things from the conference table. "How's Velvet?"

"She's doing better. Not out of the woods yet, though. She's had two transfusions, and she's on stall rest. The clinic has a couple of other foals, and Styx goes out to play with them."

"Sticks? Is that the baby? You trying to branch out with that name?"

Oh, dad jokes. I'll pretend I didn't get it so I don't encourage him. "S-t-y-x. For one thing, he's all black, and for another, the River Styx is the border between the world of the living and the world of the dead. Seemed appropriate. Poor guy. His dam's getting so much medication that he can't drink her milk. When he's in the stall with her, he has to wear a muzzle. They're bottle feeding him, though. You should see how much bigger he's gotten in a week and a half."

"I'd like to see him again. They're in good hands. Dr. Mueller's one of the best."

"I know."

They headed toward the parking lot. Jax opened the door.

"Do you want to leave your car here and ride with me?"

It would mean back-tracking from the restaurant to come back and get her car, and she still had an essay to write when she got home. Thoughtful idea, but terribly impractical.

"Sure."

He opened the truck door for her, then climbed in behind the wheel. The diesel engine growled to life. "I've never been to El Puerto Azul before. Can you navigate?"

"It's on the north side of I-10 from Memorial City Mall. East side of Gessner."

"That's easy."

Ivy had wanted to ride to the restaurant with Jax so she'd have more time to talk to him. But now she couldn't think of a single thing to say.

"Who is it we're meeting again? Jenny and Kara?"

"Julie and Karen. Julie is my partner at the rescue. No way I could do that all on my own. Karen is her... girlfriend."

"Girlfriend as in a friend who happens to be a girl, or as in someone she's dating?"

"Dating."

Jax nodded. "Am I going to be cross-examined?"

"I hope it doesn't come to that! Julie just wanted to meet you. My mom has been dead for a long time, and Julie's kind of stepped into her shoes."

"I'm sorry. About your mom."

"It was a long time ago. Cancer."

Jax reached across the seat and squeezed her hand. When he took it away to turn the corner, she instantly missed its warmth.

He steered to straddle a pothole. "It's good to have friends who care that much about you."

"I don't know what I'd do without them." Ivy stared out the window and watched headlights blur past. What would she do if Julie and Karen didn't like Jax? She couldn't bear to think about it.

"So what about you? Are you a native Houstonian?"

"Not quite. Grew up outside of Katy. Mom was a book-keeper in town. Dad was a farmer. Rice and Black Angus cattle. Been on a horse since I was four. My sister Helen, well, sometimes I wonder if the hospital sent home the wrong baby."

Ivy chuckled. "Why is that?"

"Nobody is more opposed to getting sweaty and dirty than she is. Hard to reconcile that with living on a farm."

"Yeah. Does your family still have the farm?"

Jax jammed on the brakes to avoid a red-light runner. "They still own the property. My dad's semi-retired. He's not planting rice anymore, but he does still have some cows, mostly because he just likes them. I go help him out sometimes."

It was nearly impossible to miss the blinking neon blue door on the top of the restaurant.

Ivy took a deep breath. "Looks like we're here."

It took a few turns around the parking lot before Jax found a space. It was go-time.

They approached two women—a redhead and a blonde—who sat on a wooden bench near the hostess's podium, looking over the restaurant's offerings.

Ivy tapped the closest one's menu. "Hey, we're here."

"Finally! I'm starved," the redhead said.

"Nice to see you, too, Julie." Ivy breathed in. "Julie, Karen—Jax. Jax—Julie, Karen."

Karen's blonde China doll brushed her shoulders as she tilted her head. "Jax? Is that short for anything?"

Don't let decorum get in your way.

He hesitated. "Ajax."

His sister's lucky her name isn't Comet.

Karen glanced at Julie. "One of the giant Greek heroes. Laid waste to many a Trojan."

Ivy felt her entire face go scarlet.

Karen seemed puzzled by the reaction. "What? He was known to be much larger than his peers. And famous for his huge shield that archers could hide behind while shooting a stream of arrows at the oncoming enemy."

"Thank you, Karen. I think we get the picture." Ivy turned to Jax. "Did I mention she's an ancient history professor?"

He grinned. "She's not wrong, though. My mother didn't have the money to finish college, but she was very well-read. Loved the Iliad. Hence, Ajax and Helen. I could just as easily have been Achilles."

Wonder what else she's not wrong about.

The restaurant's pager on the bench next to Julie vibrated and lit up.

The hostess led them to a large corner booth with vibrant Talavera tiles embedded in the table.

After they ordered, Julie leaned her elbows on the cool tiles and crossed her arms. "So, Jax. Tell us about yourself."

Ivy shot her a warning look, but Julie never took her eyes off Jax.

He seemed unfazed. "What would you like to know?"

"Ivy says you're a mounted patrol officer. How did you get into that?"

Ivy took too big of a sip of her margarita and the tequila burned a path straight to her brain.

He told them the Cliff Notes version of what he'd told Ivy earlier.

Julie nodded along as he talked, as if committing every detail to memory. When he finished, she looked him up and down. "Why is a man who looks like you single?"

"Julie!" Ivy slapped her hand on the table.

"It's a reasonable question. Objection overruled." She turned back to Jax.

Jax's smile didn't reach his eyes, and he tapped his thumb on the edge of the table. "My job can have pretty crazy hours. Tough to find somebody with the right personality *and* a compatible schedule."

Ivy noted the sudden tension in his shoulders. *There's more to it than that, isn't there?*

The server appeared with their food, and Ivy sighed with relief. The interrogation ground to a halt while the plates were distributed and drinks re-filled.

Julie waved her fork. "These fusion places are popping up everywhere. Have you been here before, Jax?"

Chewing, he shook his head. Once he swallowed, he said, "No, first time. Ivy said you chose the place. What do *you* think of fusion restaurants?"

Julie grinned and even Karen smiled. Julie took a sip of her choco-tini. "I love trying new places and having novel experiences." She looked at her plate and pushed some Spanish rice around. "Look, I'm sorry about the third degree. Ivy... has not had the best luck with men, and we're always trying to look out for her."

"I noticed that. She's lucky to have friends who have her back."

Karen dipped a tortilla chip in her refried beans. "What do you think of the horse rescue?"

"It's impressive. Takes a lot of hard work and dedication." He turned his head and gave Ivy a quick smile.

Ivy felt the tension flowing out of her body, but whether it was due to the heavy-handed pour of the margarita or Jax's easy way of responding to Julie's questioning she couldn't be sure.

The conversation gradually flowed into more mundane territory. Jax wheedled some teaching stories out of Karen, and Julie made sure to tell Jax about the time they'd met up for Thanksgiving and Ivy had managed to set the glazed ham on fire. But Ivy noted that he didn't volunteer much information about himself.

The check was paid, and Julie and Karen left. Ivy wanted to finish up the water she'd ordered to dilute the margarita, and even then she only drank half of it. She still had miles to go before she slept.

Jax moved his empty dinner plate out of the way. "I've heard of Cali-Mex and Tex-Mex, but fusion-Mex is new."

"What did you think?"

"The corn and refried bean samosas were weird. But the kobo beef and bok choy enchiladas were better than I expected."

"Julie loves this place—it's just like her—not what you were expecting." Ivy smiled, then yawned. "I still have to get back and write an essay."

"Do you need help with the horses?"

"Thanks, but Julie fed this evening while we were at the meeting." She put down her empty glass and stood up. "I'm planning to go to the vet's to see Velvet and Styx on Friday, after I feed."

They made their way out to the parking lot.

"Why don't I help you feed then and we can ride up there together, maybe grab something to eat on the way back?"

An untrustworthy kind of warmth bubbled up inside Ivy, making her want to do things she really, really shouldn't. At least not yet.

"We're hauling out Saturday afternoon for a training workshop in Dallas. We'll be there all week and come back the next Saturday."

Ivy forced herself to smile to cover her disappointment. "What's the workshop about?"

"New equipment, techniques, practicing drills and scenarios with other agencies, that sort of thing."

"Sounds interesting." She cringed. That hadn't come out right.

He opened the door, and she stepped up into the cab.

Jax pulled up next to her car and shifted into park. "I liked meeting Julie and Karen. They seem like good people."

"*I* think so." She unbuckled her seatbelt, needing to go, but not wanting to.

Jax got out and opened her door. He kissed her then. A soft, lingering kiss on the lips. His touch was electric. She caressed his cheek and pulled away. If she didn't, he might have to arrest her for public lewdness.

She smiled softly. "See you Friday."

Chapter
Eight

JAX WAITED UNTIL Ivy's car pulled out onto the street before he eased out of the parking spot. He could still taste her, and her perfume lingered on the seat. He almost felt drunk.

Don't get too attached—you know what happened last time.

That wasn't my fault.

Or hers.

You were driving. If you'd been paying better attention, or reacted quicker...

He turned the radio up and sang along, drowning out that voice that seemed to exist solely to suck the joy out of his life.

Jax sat in his truck for a minute after he pulled up in Ivy's driveway. *What am I doing here?* He was about to step over a line he couldn't uncross. Granted, his emotional scars might have a better chance of healing if he'd quick picking at the scabs. He missed having someone at home to talk to—Flip didn't count because those conversations were remarkably one-sided. Besides, that dog would say anything to get a rawhide bone.

He popped a piece of gum in his mouth and chewed for a few seconds, long enough for it to do its work, then spat it in the trash bag that clipped on to the middle console.

When Jax walked through the double barn doors, he saw Ivy in the enclosure with Amos, scooping racoon poop, while the critter lounged in his hammock eating grapes.

"Hey, Jax!" She collected the last two deposits and tied off the sack.

"Hey." He couldn't help grinning like an idiot.

Ivy exited the raccoon cage and disposed of her bag in the nearby bin.

Jax picked a piece of straw out of her hair and kissed her on the cheek. He liked the way she smelled of flowers, even as a fresh layer of sweat glistened on her skin.

"I need to go wash my hands. Be right back."

"Good plan."

Ivy came out of the office, wiping her hands on her pants. "I've fed, but haven't cleaned stalls yet. They've been out all day, so there shouldn't be much of anything."

She was right. One stall needed picking. When that was done, he followed her back into the office.

Ivy re-washed her hands, then pulled a vial and a box of syringes out of the mini-fridge. "Natalie cut herself yesterday. Dr. Clark came out and stitched her up, but now she's on antibiotics."

"Never a dull moment around here."

"I could go for dull sometimes."

Jax followed her to the stall of the bay mare with only one eye. Ivy eased inside, talking to the horse the entire time, and slipped a halter over the mare's head. "Could you hold her? If you scratch just under her mane, she won't even notice me back here giving her a shot."

He took the lead rope and started scratching under her black mane. Ivy jabbed the needle into Natalie's rump and pressed the plunger. A swish of the tail was the only comment the mare made about her injection.

"All done. I'll just dispose of this on the way out." Ivy put the cap back on the needle.

A few minutes later, they pulled out of the driveway in Jax's truck. He glanced at Ivy via the rearview mirror.

"Any updates on Velvet?"

"Still hanging in there. If all goes well, she can be hand-grazed in a few days. Styx can't nurse off her because of the meds, but they've been milking her every day to keep her from drying up." Ivy made a face. "Maybe that's TMI."

When they arrived at the clinic, Delta said Dr. Mueller was finishing up a surgery and would be out to talk to Ivy when she was done.

Jax watched as Ivy carefully entered Velvet's space. Styx was lying flat on his side in the middle of the double-sized foaling stall. His mother stood in the corner with her head down, flicking her ear at Ivy as she approached. The massive horse let Ivy stroke her face and even stretched her neck out a little when her withers were scratched. He was imagining her lavishing some of that attention on him and didn't notice when Dr. Mueller came up.

He startled when she said, "Today is the last dose of her Naxalone. We're going to try to get Styx back to nursing tomorrow. We did an ultrasound—it's looking good, but still too fragile for her to move around much."

Jax cleared his throat. "I think she's put on a little weight."

Ivy whirled toward him, "What? I haven't…nevermind."

Laughing, Dr. Mueller said, "That'll happen when you're standing in your stall munching hay all day. Still needs a couple of hundred pounds, though."

Jax stared at his menu without really seeing it. He didn't feel hungry, but unless he wanted to look like an idiot, going to a restaurant and not ordering food, he'd better make a decision.

The Texas blonde server returned with their iced teas. "Y'all ready?"

Ivy set down her menu. "I'd like the fettuccine Alfredo, with a side salad, please."

"Deluxe burger and tots, no onion."

"No onion," the waitress repeated. "Got it." She gathered up the laminated menus and left.

"You're very brave, ordering pasta and a salad at a truck stop." Jax fidgeted with his silverware.

Ivy flashed her crooked smile. "I've had it before. It's not bad."

"Truck stop connoisseur, are you?"

"Way too many trips to the vet."

He took a long drag on his iced tea. "Guess that's how it goes with a rescue."

"Or sometimes, just having a regular horse."

"There's that. What got you into the rescue business?" He mostly just wanted to listen to the sound of her voice.

"I used to show hunters. Hardly have time to ride anymore, though. My horse, Copper Penny, was a gorgeous, golden chestnut with lots of chrome. He won championship after championship—one in a million. On the night before the Medal Finals, someone loaded eight horses into our trailer that was packed with all of our tack for the show and took off. Security camera didn't help much—he was wearing a hat and a bandana.

"The truck and empty trailer turned up the next day at a truck stop. The horses and tack were gone. The Texas Rangers found four of them at an auction, but they never located the rest. Copper was one of the ones at the auction."

"That must have been a relief."

Ivy's eyes welled with tears. "The left him standing there in the sun on three legs. He'd been kicked by another horse, and his right hind cannon bone was shattered. Had to put him down."

"I'm so sorry. I—" He handed her a napkin. If he hadn't been so nosy, she wouldn't be crying right now.

"I couldn't pretend that I didn't know what happened to horses that went to auction after that. I save as many as I can.

Some are too broken to adopt out, but others have ended up in the show ring."

"You turned a tragedy into a cause. Most people can't do that."

"Maybe. But I would have done anything to have saved Copper. He didn't deserve what they did to him."

The waitress brought Ivy's salad. She rearranged the greens and the two cherry tomatoes with her fork.

He also wished he could have saved someone who could not be saved. How had the conversation gotten so dark?

"My sister, Helen, once rescued a crawfish."

"A crawfish?"

"Our dad was having a crawfish boil to celebrate his youngest brother getting engaged. He bought a fifty-pound sack of live crawfish. Helen didn't want them to be boiled alive and tried to drag the sack down to the rice well to turn them loose, but she couldn't budge it. There was one blue crawfish near the top of the bag, so she picked him up and put him in a bowl of water in her room."

"How long did that last?"

"It had crawled out of the bowl by the time she went to bed. Two days later, Mom was making breakfast when we heard her scream. We all ran to the kitchen to see what was wrong."

Ivy's eyes widened.

"There was Helen's crawfish, covered with dust bunnies, menacing my mother with its blue claws."

"What did you do with it?"

"Helen scooped it up in a juice glass and we took it down to the stock tank. A flick of its tail, and it was gone. Never saw it again."

Her eyelashes were still wet, but at least she gave him half a smile. He'd have to be more careful of these emotional landmines. He became aware that his thumb was tracing around the scar underneath his sleeve and quickly uncrossed his arms.

Jax walked Ivy to her door. Her dogs woofed half-heartedly on the other side a few times then quieted. He brushed a stray lock of hair out of her eyes.

"Text me while I'm gone and let me know how Velvet's doing."

"I'm glad you're so concerned about her."

Without stopping to think about it, he slipped his arms around her waist and pulled her close. Her arms twined around his neck, and he kissed her, softly, deeply. He liked the way she fit into his arms, how she was warm and soft against his chest. How her hair smelled like flowers. He wanted her, and his body responded accordingly.

Bam!

A hollow thud came from the direction of the barn, followed immediately by a yelp.

"What was that?" Ivy slipped out of his embrace and ran toward the stables.

Disappointed, Jax hurried to catch up.

Ivy snapped on the lights, and a thin white and brindle puppy cowered against a stall door. The horse on the other side kicked the door, and the puppy yelped and crouched down in the dirt aisleway.

"Where did you come from?" She reached out gingerly to let the dog sniff her fingers. The dog put its head down and screamed.

"Hey Jax? There's a bin of cat food in the feed room. Could you bring me a handful of that?"

"Sure."

As he approached Ivy with the food, the puppy started screaming again. He kneeled slowly and handed Ivy the kibble, breathing in the smell of her. Even with cat food overtones, she still smelled so very appealing.

She offered the pup a few nuggets of cat food. Hunger was stronger than fear, and eyes wide, it cautiously took the food. She doled out a few more pieces.

Keeping her eyes on the puppy, Ivy said, "There's a large crate in the tack room, underneath the shelves where the supplements are. Could you put that in the office and grab a towel from the cabinet by the sink for her to lay on?"

He got the temporary bedroom set up and came back out into the aisleway. Ivy stood, then leaned over to pick the dog up. Whimpering, the dog snapped at her when it realized what was happening. As gently as she could, she took a hold of the scruff of the puppy's neck and, supporting its weight with her other hand, lifted it up. As she passed by, he could see small round sores on the dog's belly. He'd seen them before, on child abuse cases.

Cigarette burns.

No wonder the dog was terrified of people.

"Little girl. I'll take her to Dr. Garabaldi in the morning."

They started back toward the house. "How well do you know your neighbors, Ivy?" *Because people who do these things to animals often graduate to humans.*

"I don't think any of them would torture a dog, if that's what you're getting at. Poor thing was probably dumped."

Maybe she was right. Something was wrong here—he could feel it in his gut. But he had no idea what it was.

Ivy stopped and turned to him. "Do you want to come in for a while?"

Nothing I want to do more. "I have to go. Have to get up at three, because we're hauling out at four thirty."

Ivy's face fell.

"But I will take a rain check when I get back."

"Sure."

She brightened again, and he kissed her goodbye.

After he pulled out of her driveway and turned the bend away from her house, he saw a red pickup with its hazards on. He took his Glock out of the glove box and pushed it into his pocket, untucking his shirt to cover the grip before he got out of his own truck. He also grabbed his heavy flashlight.

"You okay? Need any help?"

A scruffy man stood up from where he'd been squatting by the back wheel. Greasy, dishwater blond hair clumped around his face. "Naw, I'm good. Had a flat, just tightenin' up the lugs."

Jax shone the light around, just to make sure there wasn't anyone else lurking in the dark, waiting to ambush him. The two men were alone, at least as far as he could tell. "You want me to shine the light for you while you finish so you don't get run over?"

"Sure, man."

In less than two minutes, the job was done, and Jax followed the red truck back to the main road. He wished he was on duty, so he could run the guy's plates. Just in case.

On Wednesday, Jax skipped the hotel's continental breakfast. Ruby had been acting a little off, and he wanted to check on her before the parade workshop started. As he was getting in his truck, he got a text from Jesse, the groom. "We have a situation. Get here ASAP"

Jax arrived at the stables less than ten minutes later. Most of the stall doors were open, not just for his group, but for other agencies as well. Some horses nervously snatched at grass near the wash racks, and others ran around bucking and squealing. One large white horse that Jax didn't recognize trotted around shaking his head and neck, trying to separate some horses from the herd and threatening others. Thick jaw. Heavy crest. The horse paused to let out a throaty scream.

Jax shook his head. *Where did that stallion come from?*

Three men with halters, one of them holding a feed bucket, futilely tried to close in on him. He raised his tail, shook his head and trotted away, extending his stride as he went so it looked like his hooves didn't even touch the ground as he circled a group of perhaps ten horses.

"Nice mover," Jax said, half out loud.

"*We* think so." A woman with close-cropped grey hair stood a dozen feet from him. "I'm Elaine, from Montmartre Farms. That's Sacre Coeur, our top show jumping stallion. I'm really sorry about the escape. He's bad about opening doors, and we have a new guy who forgot to put the snap in the latch after he cleaned stalls."

"I see."

Ruby's chestnut head popped up in the small herd of mares Sacre Coeur was trying to claim as his harem. From where Jax stood, she appeared to be okay, but he wasn't about to go near her until the stallion was captured.

Mm. Mm. Maaaa.

A young woman led a black goat up the drive. Sacre Coeur stopped and whinnied.

Maaaa. Maaaa.

Mares forgotten, he cantered to the goat and began to nuzzle along its back. One of the men with a halter slipped it over the big horse's head and led him away, goat at his side.

"That's his pet goat, Billie. Loves that goat more than anything. Again, I'm really sorry for the mayhem." Elaine handed him a card and left.

The mares didn't seem especially disappointed that the stallion was being led away, and if any of them felt slighted that she'd been thrown over for a goat, she didn't let on. The group munched happily on the available greenery until, one by one, they were haltered and led back to their accommodations.

Whatever had been bothering Ruby before had stopped—she was back to her usual self the rest of the week. At least, that's what Jax told himself.

Chapter
Nine

IVY NEEDED ANOTHER dog like she needed a hole in her head. Flash. That's what she named the puppy that turned up just in time to crush her romantic moment with Jax. The pup desperately needed socialization, and she wasn't going to get it sitting in a cage in the vet's office, or in a shelter somewhere. The burns would heal soon enough. The mental scars? Only time would tell on those, and the more positive experiences she had, the better.

Ivy folded her Sunday afternoon laundry, watching Eddie and Flash chase each other around the yard. Twilight supervised. Maybe it's just as well. If Flash hadn't appeared when she did, would she have slept with Jax? What if that was really all he wanted from her? How big a mistake that would have been! When she'd found out what Chance had been up to, she'd sworn off men. She had more than enough on her plate, and who needed the hassle of a romance that was just going to crash and burn, anyway?

And yet...

When she was around Jax, she felt a lot of things—safe, giddy, desirable. Which was all well and good, but was it necessary? She could take care of herself (the one time she'd needed it, her pepper spray had worked just fine), and was giddy such a good thing?

But when he kissed her, and she was surrounded by the heat of his body and the strength of his arms, she craved more. It was also true that sometimes she craved chocolate cake, and that didn't mean that she should give in to her sweet tooth every time.

Flash yelped. Ivy looked up and saw her tearing toward the house with her tail tucked between her legs. Eddie was staring at the thin strip of thicket that stood between her house and her neighbor's. Even Twilight stood up, raising her head for a better view.

Unease slithered down her spine and coiled, purring, in her midsection. Eddie hasn't found another skunk, has he?

Ivy stepped onto her porch and called the dogs, "Eddie! Twilight! Come!"

Eddie looked at her, then crashed back into the bushes.

"Eddie! Come here!"

The white dog barked twice and trotted towards the house, turning to scan the trees a few times on the way.

Twilight observed the woods until Eddie was almost to the porch. Then she made her own way to the door. Flash had bolted into the house and hidden under the bed while the other two were still investigating.

The two horses grazing in the field nearby looked up and studied the shrubbery for a moment when Eddie barked. One snorted, and they both moved toward the gate. Ivy locked the door as soon as the dogs were in, grateful that Julie and Karen were stopping by in a little while with takeout.

On Wednesday evening, Ivy texted Jax the news that Velvet could be hand grazed for fifteen minutes a day. He'd said he wanted updates while he was gone. She'd wanted to text him every day, but she stopped herself. She missed him more than she should have, given the short time she'd known him. And if he knew that...well, Chance was never above using her feelings against her. Better safe than sorry.

Sunday brunch at the Enamel Trivet was always a treat. When Jax had called late Saturday afternoon and asked if she wanted to get together for Sunday brunch, it seemed like the obvious choice. Mimosas weren't included, so that kept it affordable, at least for Ivy, anyway.

Watching a giggling young lady in stilettos wobble by, Ivy was happy about her mimosa-free meal. It was funny, until she noticed Jax staring at the woman with hard eyes, not looking away until she disappeared into the ladies' room. Ivy took a sip of coffee and shifted in her seat. Police were supposed to keep drunk drivers off the road, weren't they? That's all it was. The look on his face was disgust, not desire.

"So. Tell me more about your conference. We've been talking about Velvet and Styx almost the whole time."

"It was good. Saw some old friends, learned some new stuff..."

"But nothing really happened."

Jax picked up a croissant. "Not exactly nothing. On Wednesday, a stallion from two farms away got loose and came by the stables to let the horses out."

"A stallion!" Ivy almost dropped her fork. "Is Ruby okay?"

"She's fine—just had an unscheduled turnout. She's on a progesterone supplement."

"Your horse is on the pill?"

The croissant now a memory, he raised his coffee cup. "For just such occurrences. I can't be riding a pregnant mare around on patrol, now can I?"

His grin was infectious, and Ivy couldn't help grinning back. But that was really enough birth control talk. No telling where that conversation might lead if it was allowed to go further. She had to change the subject, and pronto.

"Have you had much time to think about the gala?"

"The gala...yes. I think Katherine has the decorating nailed down, and Hillary's got the DJ lined up. The other three can help out with the decorating and run the raffle. I was thinking that maybe you and I could work the registration desk. People will come in, give us their tickets, and we'll show them where their tables are on the seating chart. Shouldn't take more than an hour—thirty minutes before, and thirty minutes into the event."

"And then what?" It could be a very long night if there wasn't anything to do.

"As the Chairman of the Welcoming Committee, I would have to make sure that everyone feels welcome. That would include testing the dance floor and quality control checks on the appetizers."

"Is that what they're calling raiding the buffet these days?"

"Shhh. Don't tell my sister." He winked at her.

Ivy mimed pulling a zipper across her lips. She didn't think she could force another morsel into her mouth. But she didn't want to leave. Three papers and a slide show waited at home for her, all due tomorrow. Sometimes she wished she hadn't decided to go back to school. But it would be worth it when the ordeal was over. At least that's what she kept telling herself. What was that saying? If you're going through hell, keep going! It would have been so much more pleasant to sit next to Jax and make plans for the gala.

Maybe there was room for another small glass of orange juice.

Two weeks flew by. Karen had loaned her a dress to wear to the gala, but Ivy wished that Julie and Karen would be at the event. Although, to be honest, there was no competition between a charity kick-off gala and a Caribbean cruise. Ivy suspected that her business partner was going to pop the question, and she couldn't imagine a better match for Julie than Karen. Briefly, Ivy wondered what her life would be like if she'd met Jax instead of Chance three years ago, and if her need to rescue broken creatures would doom her to forever choose the wrong kind of man. Jax didn't talk about his past, other than the occasional childhood tale. That was fine for now, but Ivy couldn't help but wonder what might be lurking there.

She pulled into a parking space at the Bennington Hotel. This was it. The big night. She checked her teeth in the rearview mirror, dabbed a little more powder on her nose, and took a deep breath. Then opened the car door.

Getting into the car with a long skirt and heels hadn't been too bad. Getting out of the car with all that fabric was a different story. She was glad she'd had to sense to wear low heels, but they still caught in the hem of her floor-length skirt as she tried to swing her legs out of the seat. Frustrated, she hiked the dress up to mid-thigh and stepped onto the asphalt. A parking valet stood near the kiosk and watched her, obviously amused by her predicament and ultimate solution. He probably didn't notice the icicles she glared at him through the murky twilight, but it made her feel better, anyway.

The hotel was buzzing with people, most of them in evening wear. Were they all here for the gala? She was forty-five minutes early, and it seemed like half the guests had arrived before her. She hurried down the corridor to the Diamond Room—the main ballroom.

Jax stood behind an elegantly draped table, arranging swag bags. In his perfectly tailored black tux, he looked like a movie star. Ivy suddenly felt underdressed. Couldn't change her outfit now, so she breathed deep, squared her shoulders, and smiled.

"Hey, Jax."

He looked up, and a grin spread across his face. Ivy glanced over her shoulder. No one was behind her.

"Ivy! You look... amazing."

"Thanks. You clean up pretty good yourself."

He gazed at her for just a heartbeat too long. "We have these gift bags. One per couple. If you, um, want to hand them out, I can show them where to sit."

Ivy walked around to his side of the table and stood just inside the edge of his personal space. He took a step closer to her.

"Ahem!"

They both looked up to see Ashley Smith peering out of the ballroom at them. "Can you find the hotel's AV guy? Simon is having some trouble with the sound system."

Who is Simon? "Is that the DJ?"

Ashley pursed her lips. "Yes. Hillary's nephew. We can't have a ball without music, now can we?"

"I'm on it." Jax strode down the corridor toward the front desk.

Ivy wasn't sure if she should stay at the table and guard the goodie bags, or if it would be okay to take a peek inside the ballroom. She knew that Katherine Edgemont had arranged a battalion of volunteers to decorate, and they'd been at it all day.

A woman with two small children hurried towards her. The kids rushed to the table, eyes on the decorated bags.

"These for everybody?" the woman asked.

At least she asked. "No, I'm sorry. These are for the gala guests."

The little girl looked at Ivy, then her eyes got big. "Are you a princess?"

"Me? I'm—"

"Of course she is, Maddie." The mom winked at Ivy. "You can tell all your friends at pre-K that you got to meet a real princess on your trip."

The little girl made an awkward curtsy and skipped down the hall, her brother running after her.

"Walk, please!" The mother hurried after them.

Jax returned with the AV engineer, and they disappeared into the ballroom. A couple of minutes later, she heard some blasts of music from the speakers. And not a moment too soon—the first attendees were making their way down the corridor.

For forty-five minutes, Ivy and Jax checked in and ushered guests as fast as decorum would allow. A handful of couples straggled in over the next half hour.

Jax pored over the guest list. "I think everybody that's coming is here. You want to join the party?"

"But of course!"

He held out his arm, and she took it. She smiled—perhaps too much—and focused her attention on walking because her knees had gone wobbly.

Katherine was the Pinterest queen. Instead of a generic hotel ballroom, Ivy and Jax walked into an autumn forest lit with floating balls of light. The cash bar was nestled into an arbor twined with orange flowering vines. Clusters of tables with silent auction items were scattered throughout the room, dressed as boulders. Blue lights projected rippling water onto the dance floor.

"Canape?" The tuxedoed waiter, brandishing a silver tray, broke the spell.

They each took a skewer of cheese cube, tomato, and olive.

Ivy shook her head as she looked around the room again. The buffet table was covered in Astroturf sprinkled with plastic daisies.

She turned back to Jax. "Incredible."

He didn't look at anything but her. "Yes."

It was suddenly hard for Ivy to breathe.

Over the microphone, the ching-ching-ching of a knife tapping on a water glass. "Ladies and gentlemen, the buffet is now available. Please feel free to make your silent auction bids throughout the evening. We'll be collecting them at eleven."

Ivy hadn't noticed the classical music playing softly in the background until it wasn't there. She caught a glimpse of a young man sequestered behind a wishing well. Must be Simon, the DJ. Eine Kleine Nachtmusik resumed.

A willowy blonde in a blue-sequined gown with a plunging neckline approached, an older man with a sapphire bowtie in tow. Ivy recognized her from the planning kick off meeting. The woman put her arms around Jax's neck and kissed the air near his cheek.

"This decorating is amazing. Who is responsible for this? I want to hire her!" She gazed at Ivy.

"This is Ivy Stonewall. She's on my committee, but not the decorator. Ivy, this is my sister, Helen, and her husband, Morgan."

Ivy nodded to both of them. "Nice to meet you."

"Charmed," Morgan replied. Nothing overt, but a flicker of rapacity in his eyes made Ivy take a step backward. It was gone so fast she couldn't be sure it wasn't her imagination.

Helen only smiled.

Jax took Ivy's hand. "Come on, Helen. Let's introduce you to Katherine."

Ivy spotted her on the opposite side of the ballroom, and they made their way over, Helen or Morgan stopping to greet one couple or another along the way.

Once the introductions were made, Jax turned to Ivy. "Are you ready for something to eat?"

"I'm starved."

The food was good, what little Ivy was able to swallow. Butterflies flapped hard against her stomach. Then the music started.

"Shall we?"

"I've never really done ballroom dancing before." Ivy fidgeted with her napkin.

Jax stood and held out his hand. "Helen drags me to these things all the time. Most of the people on the floor don't know how to ballroom dance, either."

Ivy was starting to feel a little chilled, and Jax's warm hand on the small of her back felt especially good. When they got to the dance floor, he faced her, leaving one arm around her waist, and took her other hand in his own. He actually knew what he was doing on the floor, and at first Ivy struggled to keep up. Once she got comfortable following his lead, she began to relax. She wasn't sure if it was the heat of his body or the spicy citrus scent of his cologne that went straight to her head and made her feel a little dizzy.

It was 11:45. They'd danced their way through classical, country, smooth jazz, and some 80s hits. The hotel staff was starting to congregate near the doors to swoop in and clear away the setup. The music stopped. The silent auction winners were announced and items awarded.

After they cleaned up the welcome table, Jax walked Ivy to her car. He kissed her. She kissed him back, urgently. He kissed her jaw, then whispered, "Do you want—"

Jax's text chime went off. His shoulders slumped. "I have to take this. Hold on."

His face went white as he read the message.

"Jax? What's wrong?"

"I have to go. I'll call you later." He gave her a quick peck on the lips and jogged to his truck.

Chapter
Ten

THIS WAS THE text that Jax had been dreading.

He pushed the light. It was...orange. A driver in a Honda beeped at him, but he didn't care. He had to get to the barn, and he wished he was in a squad car so he could hit the lights, and no one would question his speed.

Jax had gone to see his retired horse in the afternoon before the gala. Murphy had been standing in his paddock, snoozing in the sun. He'd barely flicked an ear when Jax called him. Usually he came trotting up, eager for cookies. Nothing else seemed amiss, though, at least not until Jax stopped by Murphy's stall to check on his salt block. About half of the horse's breakfast was still in the feeder. He usually counted his pellets and complained if he felt shorted.

Jax asked the on-site stable manager, Kim, to check on Murphy before she went to bed. Seeing Ivy in that curve-hugging dress had pushed his worries to the sidelines. Until he got Kim's text.

"Murphy colicking. Vet otw."

Colic. Is it just gas, or will it be fatal? The question haunted every horse owner's thoughts at one point or another.

Jax whipped around a slow-moving minivan and punched it, just making it through the light. *I'm coming, Murph. Wait for me.*

Memories swirled in his head as he drove. Jax had gotten five-year-old Murphy for a 4H project when he was in sixth grade. He still had that faded third-place ribbon somewhere.

The bay horse had been around through everything for more than half of Jax's life. Helen had taken care of him for the two years Jax was in the army.

It was through his post-college riding renaissance that he'd met Elise. She'd been half-leasing Murphy while Jax was finishing his degree, and he'd fallen hard for her the first time he saw her riding his horse in the arena. It wasn't just the way she looked in form-fitting riding pants. Her hands were soft on the reins, and she lavished praise on her equine partner at every opportunity. They'd joked about Murphy being the best man at their wedding. And he almost was. He was the horse that Fallon, their two-year-old daughter, won lead-line classes on.

And he was there when the sky fell in and threatened to drown Jax in grief.

The horse was a bit creaky, but he was sound enough to go on short trail rides through the wooded pastures of the stables. Whether it was his calming energy or the long-term bond they shared, Murphy was the only thing that kept Jax going during those dark days. Murphy was the one constant in the mutable sea that was life.

Jax growled as a BMW pulled partway into the intersection, blocking the lane, blocking Jax's progress. *Where's a cop when you need one?*

Finally, the gate to the farm hove into view. The barn lights were on—usually a sign of evening lessons or early morning show preparations. But not at midnight. At this hour, it meant a sick or injured horse.

Fear.

Pain.

Death.

Gravel crunched under the tires as he pulled into the drive. His hands shook as he turned the wheel, and his stomach clenched hard around the fancy gala food he'd eaten earlier. Parking the truck and hurrying down the barn aisle was a blur. Only seeing Murphy standing in the treatment stanchion, head hanging, brought reality into crisp focus.

An IV bag hung on a pole, tubing taped to the horse's neck. He was soaked in sweat, and his ribs rose and fell too fast. Pulling off a disposable exam glove that went all the way to his shoulder, Dr. Clark looked grim in the sallow light. Kim stood next to Murphy, stroking his neck.

"How is he?" Jax already knew it was bad. Before he saw the pain in the horse's eyes. Before he laid his hand on Murphy's shoulder and felt cold skin.

"It's a twist. I'm so sorry."

A twisted intestine. Fatal without surgery. Surgery that a horse Murphy's age would never survive.

"Jax?" Dr. Clark prompted. "What do you want to do? Let me give him some Banamine to make him more comfortable while you decide."

While the vet pulled up the injection, Jax took Murphy's face in his hands. The horse pressed his head against Jax's shoulder. Hot liquid rolled down the man's cheeks. His father's voice in his head: *Boys don't cry*. He didn't care. Murphy was ready to go, but Jax wanted just a little more time. He moved to the side and put his arms around the old horse's neck, resting his head on Murphy's withers.

Dr. Clark injected the Banamine. Before he'd even pulled the needle out, Murphy's legs crumpled, and he collapsed. Jax went with him.

"It looks like he made the decision for us," Dr. Clark said.

"No!" Jax wasn't ready.

But Murphy was gone, and he was now adrift.

Jax had Sunday off. He would have slept in, if he'd been able to sleep. There was no guilt this time. No, this death was routine, predictable. Sad, but inevitable.

Flip whined to go out and do his doggie business, so Jax opened the back door for him. The coffee maker gurgled. It always came on at 6:30 AM, and Jax hadn't thought to cancel the program when he came home at 3 AM. It was okay. He needed the liquid sleep.

He scrambled a couple of eggs, more from force of habit than hunger. Jax pushed them around his plate until they got cold, staring at the news feed on his phone without comprehending it. Jax gave up and scraped the eggs into Flip's bowl. He poured himself a cup of black coffee and sat out on his back deck. The house was older, on a large, wooded lot that took up most of an acre. Chinese tallows were just starting to change into their fall wardrobes. The other trees were in denial, clinging to deep summer green. A neighbor's chicken wandered across the yard. Flip barked at it, then border collie instincts kicked in and he tried to herd the nonplussed bird. The indignant hen squawked and clumsily flapped up to perch on the fence.

Jax's unfocused eyes rested on the chicken. A few hours ago, his oldest friend had passed from this earth and taken a big chunk of his heart with him. The pain wasn't just emotional—his chest was tight and his skin hurt. And now? Nothing. He dug his thumbnail into the flesh of his forearm, just a couple of inches below the palm, until it left a furrow. He saw the mark form, felt the pressure. His gaze shifted to the angry red crescent on his wrist. No pain.

He'd known Murphy was old, and old things die. His brain understood life cycles and the inevitability of mortality.

His heart did not.

It saw only another gaping hole. Jax had Murphy so long that the horse had made his way into his owner's DNA. He'd been there when Jax's mother died. He'd been there after the accident. He didn't talk, didn't question anything. Jax could talk (or not) and Murphy would keep all his secrets.

The horse would never have told anyone about the time Jax had sat in his stall for over an hour, his service weapon in his hand, trying to think of reasons not to stare down the barrel and pull the trigger. He'd been driving. He should have hit the brake harder, or turned sharper, or floored it. Something. There had to have been something that could have prevented the accident, but he'd failed to do it.

At the funeral, Jax had sat like a lump of stone, eyes anywhere but on the toddler-sized coffin, because it was too much to bear. He couldn't look at Elise's closed white casket, either. All he could see was her eyes from the night of the accident, open and staring at nothing, blood covering her face.

Eventually, Murphy had nuzzled his hair and licked his cheek, loosening the grip of those dark memories. Jax got up and gave him a cookie. Actually, a whole handful of cookies. He'd cried then, deep wracking sobs muffled in Murphy's thick mane. Murphy had pulled him back from the brink.

And now he was gone.

Jax's phone buzzed in his pocket, startling him. He didn't know how long he'd been staring into space, but Flip was curled by his feet and his coffee was cold. It was a text from Ivy.

"You ok?"

No, not really. Still, he could go see her. Maybe she would let him make love to her, lose himself in the feel of her body, the scent of her hair. But she might also say no. He couldn't risk rejection right now.

He texted back. "Call you soon."

Soon being relative.

After the accident, the department shrink had recommended journaling. He hadn't journaled, so much as he'd written letters to his dead wife. He hadn't done it for some time now. There seemed nothing left to say.

He got up and pulled some paper out of the printer tray, located a pen, and sat down at the table.

Dear Elise:

I'm sure you already know this, but Murphy died very early this morning. He's probably already come to you looking for cookies. Give him as many as he wants-he was the best.

It's been a while since I've written to you. Hope you and Fallon are doing well, and that there are endless dandelions for her to scatter on the breeze. I don't know what there is to do in Paradise-maybe you've figured out how to knit that hat you always said you were going to learn to make. I'm looking forward to seeing it.

Miss you,

Jax

Chapter
Eleven

"H ELLO?" IVY DIDN'T recognize the number. She set her pen
down on the textbook.

"Ivy?"

"Who's asking?"

"Darling, it's Helen Butterfield. I need a huge favor."

Did this have to do with the gala? Had we forgotten something?
"What is it?"

"I don't know if you've talked to Jax since the gala."

"I—"

"You knew he had a geriatric horse, right?"

"Yes, but—"

"Murphy died last night."

"Oh. I'm so—"

"Jax was really attached to that horse. He won't return my
calls, and I'm concerned about him. I'm in New York. Flew
out early this morning. Would you be a dear and run by his
house to see how he's doing?"

"I guess—"

"Thank you so much!"

"Helen? Why are you calling me? Surely there must be—"

"Because there's something in the way his eyes light up
when you're around. I haven't seen that sparkle in a long

"Helen called me."

"Figures. Come on in."

The black and white dog didn't stand up, but his tail thumped on the floor.

"That's Flip."

Ivy crouched and held out her hand, palm up. He made a study of it with his nose. Flip continued his investigation, and she stole a glance at Jax. His eyes were puffy and his skin was grey. Stubble littered his cheeks.

"You look awful. Did you sleep at all?"

"Not really. Free."

The dog stood up and busily sniffed at Ivy's shoes and pant legs.

She shifted her weight. "I'm really sorry to hear about Murphy."

"Thanks." Jax looked down at himself. "I just got out of the shower, and I need to run back upstairs for a sec. Just... make yourself at home." He gestured toward the sofa. "Be right back."

Ivy sat on the couch and patted Flip while she waited. The room was spartan and tidy. She had the feeling it was less meticulously tended and more ruthlessly scrubbed. It made her think of sale houses staged for viewing, all personal photos and effects hidden away. It was unusual. But she had the impending trip to the hospital for her brain to gnaw on, and it couldn't work on two problems at once.

Jax returned, fixing the collar of his blue polo shirt. His damp hair had been combed back, out of his face.

time. I can't believe you haven't noticed that." She gave Ivy the address and hung up.

Ivy didn't really have time to drive out to Jax's place and check on him. But she wouldn't be able to concentrate on her homework until she made sure he was okay. She typed the address into her navigation app and filled her travel mug with the last of the coffee. It was hard to lose a horse, especially one that had been a member of the family for such a long time.

She put Flash in her crate for the house's protection and locked the door. Ivy had only just pulled out of the driveway when her phone interrupted the navigator. She didn't need help to get out of her neighborhood, anyway. She took the call, her stomach knotting.

"Janelle?"

"I don't know how to say it, Ivy, so I'll just come out with it. MawMaw had a stroke last night. She's in ICU at Ben Taub."

"I am so sorry to hear that."

"Ya'll was close when you was married to Chance. Maw-Maw, she's forgot the last two years of her life. She was cryin' cuz you wadn't at the hospital."

Ivy had never understood how MawMaw and Chance Buchanan were related. She was one of the nicest people on the face of the Earth. And he...wasn't. Maybe he and her real child had been mixed up at the hospital.

"Ivy?"

"Sorry. Of course, I'll come see her. But I've got something else I have to do first. If I text you when I'm in the parking lot, could you take your brother down to the cafeteria or somewhere?"

"Yeah. Sure. She's in ICU, so she cain't have nothin', if you was thinkin' of gettin' her flowers or sumthin'."

Ivy had been.

"And she cain't eat nothin', neither—she got all kinda tubes in her."

"Okay. It will be awhile though, like a couple of hours. Maybe longer."

"I'll be here."

Ivy thought of her former mother-in-law, confused and hurting in the hospital bed, and it stung. Stung enough to draw tears. Losing MawMaw as family had been even more painful than Chance's betrayal. But she'd needed a clean break. It wasn't possible to hold on to MawMaw and completely let go of Chance. The last thing she needed or wanted right now was to step back into Buchanan family politics. Especially if MawMaw now thought she was still married to Chance. He would take any advantage of the situation he could, Ivy was sure of it.

She lingered at the next stop sign to re-activate the navigator. She focused on what she would say to Jax when she got to his house. Ivy wasn't familiar with the northeast side of town, other than rare trips to the airport. Even with the smug British lady badgering her from the phone, she still missed the last turn to Jax's house and had to turn around in someone's driveway. A brindle dog the size of a pony came out to bark at her. She hoped there were no more like him roaming the neighborhood.

At last, she found it. The house wasn't large, but it was on a large lot. The building was a Craftsman-style bungalow. Concrete and brick pillars held up the awning that covered the wide front porch. Matching bricks formed the chimney on the left side of the house. Two grand pecan trees shaded the front yard. A flagstone path led from the wrought-iron gate to the front steps.

Looking around for loose dogs before she opened her door, Ivy pulled in a deep breath and let it out. Other than an obese fox squirrel under one of the pecans, there were no animals that she could see.

She had expected the gate to be noisy. Didn't all wrought-iron gates creak? But this one opened silently on well-oiled hinges. Ivy smiled to herself. Only Jax's gate.

As she moved into the yard, the squirrel lumbered to the tree trunk and shinnied up the bark to a low limb, where it paused to swear at her. Ivy felt awkward as she climbed, uninvited, the four stairs up to the front porch. *Was this really a good idea? He had said he'd call her later. What if he just wanted to be left alone?*

Ivy hesitated. Somewhere inside, a dog barked. No turning back now. She rang the bell. A figure moved behind the beveled glass of the front door. The dog was barking louder now, moving closer.

The door cracked open. "Sit!"

The barking stopped, and the door opened all the way.

"Ivy? What are you doing here?"

Jax stood in front of her, wearing an undershirt and shorts. Water dripped from his hair, speckling the fab

"Can I offer you anything to drink?"

Ivy rose and moved to meet him.

"No. I'm good."

His eyes were dark with pain.

It made her heart ache. "Are you okay? Is there anything I can do?"

He held her gaze, as if he was considering her offer very carefully. Impulsively, she stepped closer and slipped her arms around his neck. He wrapped his arms around her waist and pulled her body tight against his. She stood there and breathed in the spicy citrus of his cologne, savoring the feel of his body against hers. Even the guilt that prickled her—she should not be enjoying this so much when he was suffering—didn't make her pull away. She had her own crisis waiting for her at Ben Taub hospital and being wrapped in his arms made that seem very far away. Eventually, he released her.

Eyes closed, he rested his forehead on hers for a moment. Then he moved back and took her face in both of his hands. His eyes had softened some.

"I appreciate you coming by. I really do. Don't take this personally—it's not you. I just need to be alone."

Ivy nodded. On some level, she understood that he needed to grieve in his own way. But the rejection still hurt.

"Call me if you need anything."

He kissed her softly on the forehead. Another rejection.

"I will."

Ivy turned to leave, unshed tears stinging her eyes. She slammed the car door and then hit the accelerator a little harder than she intended, scattering gravel on the road.

I hope Jax didn't see that! Don't be such a baby, Ivy. Good grief! She fumbled in the door pocket for a napkin to blot her eyes. She couldn't show up to MawMaw's hospital room looking so pitiful, so she pulled into the first coffee shop she spotted. Ivy stopped in the ladies' room to splash cold water on her face before she ordered her drink. An extra shot of espresso should shore her up to step into the grasping arms of the Buchanan clan.

Ivy passed Chance's red truck as she prowled the parking garage, looking for a spot. She was not remotely surprised to see that he'd parked just badly enough to make the space on the driver's side of his truck unusable, except for maybe a Smart Car or a motorcycle. *Some things never change.*

She found a spot three levels up, near the elevators. She texted Janelle before she got out of the car, asking her former sister-in-law to run interference with Chance. Ivy hoped that her ex had no idea she was coming, because if he did, Janelle would be no help at all. She wasn't dishonest—she just wasn't the brightest bulb in the marquee. Then again, for all Ivy knew, Chance had put his sister up to calling in the first place. Ivy shook her head. If MawMaw was on death's door and asking to see her, she'd risk having to shove Chance out of the way to do it.

She caught a whiff of Jax's cologne, wafting up from her clothes. She remembered the feel of his arms around her and got out of the car.

Her phone chimed. It couldn't send the text message. She'd have to stand outside, away from all the concrete, and hope that Janelle could get her text inside the hospital. Ivy hadn't considered this when she'd come up with her Chance-removal plan. She re-sent the text and hoped for the best.

To kill some time and give Janelle an opportunity for getting Chance out of the way (assuming she got the text), Ivy stopped in the ladies' room. She splashed more cold water on her blotchy face and patted it dry. The eyeliner pencil in her purse had just enough crayon to fix the gaps without scraping her eyelid too badly. Ivy glanced at her watch. Hopefully, eight minutes was enough. She gave her hair a final fluff and headed toward the elevator.

The tiny ICU waiting room was stuffed with Buchanans. Some glared at Ivy as soon as she rounded the corner. Avoiding eye contact with her former relations, Ivy homed in on her ex-sister-in-law, who was playing with her phone.

"Janelle?"

"Ivy! MawMaw'll be so glad to see you. Chance and Daddy's in there now."

"I thought we had a deal." Ivy hissed as she plonked down onto the hard plastic chair next to Janelle. "You said you would get Chance out of the way for me."

"What was I s'posed to do? Tell him he cain't see his momma?" She leaned back in her seat and put one hand on her belly.

"Ivy? What you doin' here, Baby Girl?" Chance stood in the doorway with his father, grinning like a 'possum eating persimmons.

She tried to squelch her anger. "I'm here to see Maw-Maw." *Not you.*

"Nurse is in there. She'll be done soon." Papa Buchanan's gravelly voice was hardly more than a whisper.

He looked so miserable that Ivy wanted to give him a big hug and tell him everything would be all right. But she was here to see MawMaw, just this once. It was a bad idea to pick up broken attachments—it would just make everything worse when they broke again at the end of this visit. Ivy just nodded.

Usually, only two visitors at a time are allowed in the ICU, so she turned to Janelle to ask her to escort her in to see Maw-Maw. *You've put on some weight. Especially around the middle.* Then it hit her.

"Janelle, are you...?"

"Yep. Six and a half months." She grinned.

"Congratulations. You've been wanting a baby for as long as I've known you."

"Lil Hank finally said he was ready. Didn't take no time after that."

A woman in hot pink scrubs stepped into the waiting area. "Alright, Mr. Buchanan. I'm all done. You can go back in now."

"Thank you, Kelly. Chance, why don't you take Ivy into see your ma?"

Ivy's jaw clenched, but she stood up and followed her ex down the short corridor to the ICU ward. MawMaw was frail and grey against the crisp white sheets and pale blue blanket. Monitor leads crept out of her hospital gown and attached themselves to a large machine. An IV stand held up three dif-

time. I can't believe you haven't noticed that." She gave Ivy the address and hung up.

Ivy didn't really have time to drive out to Jax's place and check on him. But she wouldn't be able to concentrate on her homework until she made sure he was okay. She typed the address into her navigation app and filled her travel mug with the last of the coffee. It was hard to lose a horse, especially one that had been a member of the family for such a long time.

She put Flash in her crate for the house's protection and locked the door. Ivy had only just pulled out of the driveway when her phone interrupted the navigator. She didn't need help to get out of her neighborhood, anyway. She took the call, her stomach knotting.

"Janelle?"

"I don't know how to say it, Ivy, so I'll just come out with it. MawMaw had a stroke last night. She's in ICU at Ben Taub."

"I am so sorry to hear that."

"Ya'll was close when you was married to Chance. Maw-Maw, she's forgot the last two years of her life. She was cryin' cuz you wadn't at the hospital."

Ivy had never understood how MawMaw and Chance Buchanan were related. She was one of the nicest people on the face of the Earth. And he...wasn't. Maybe he and her real child had been mixed up at the hospital.

"Ivy?"

"Sorry. Of course, I'll come see her. But I've got something else I have to do first. If I text you when I'm in the parking lot, could you take your brother down to the cafeteria or somewhere?"

"Yeah. Sure. She's in ICU, so she cain't have nothin', if you was thinkin' of gettin' her flowers or sumthin'."

Ivy had been.

"And she cain't eat nothin', neither—she got all kinda tubes in her."

"Okay. It will be awhile though, like a couple of hours. Maybe longer."

"I'll be here."

Ivy thought of her former mother-in-law, confused and hurting in the hospital bed, and it stung. Stung enough to draw tears. Losing MawMaw as family had been even more painful than Chance's betrayal. But she'd needed a clean break. It wasn't possible to hold on to MawMaw and completely let go of Chance. The last thing she needed or wanted right now was to step back into Buchanan family politics. Especially if MawMaw now thought she was still married to Chance. He would take any advantage of the situation he could, Ivy was sure of it.

She lingered at the next stop sign to re-activate the navigator. She focused on what she would say to Jax when she got to his house. Ivy wasn't familiar with the northeast side of town, other than rare trips to the airport. Even with the smug British lady badgering her from the phone, she still missed the last turn to Jax's house and had to turn around in someone's driveway. A brindle dog the size of a pony came out to bark at her. She hoped there were no more like him roaming the neighborhood.

At last, she found it. The house wasn't large, but it was on a large lot. The building was a Craftsman-style bungalow. Concrete and brick pillars held up the awning that covered the wide front porch. Matching bricks formed the chimney on the left side of the house. Two grand pecan trees shaded the front yard. A flagstone path led from the wrought-iron gate to the front steps.

Looking around for loose dogs before she opened her door, Ivy pulled in a deep breath and let it out. Other than an obese fox squirrel under one of the pecans, there were no animals that she could see.

She had expected the gate to be noisy. Didn't all wrought-iron gates creak? But this one opened silently on well-oiled hinges. Ivy smiled to herself. Only Jax's gate.

As she moved into the yard, the squirrel lumbered to the tree trunk and shinnied up the bark to a low limb, where it paused to swear at her. Ivy felt awkward as she climbed, un-invited, the four stairs up to the front porch. *Was this really a good idea? He had said he'd call her later. What if he just wanted to be left alone?*

Ivy hesitated. Somewhere inside, a dog barked. No turning back now. She rang the bell. A figure moved behind the beveled glass of the front door. The dog was barking louder now, moving closer.

The door cracked open. "Sit!"

The barking stopped, and the door opened all the way.

"Ivy? What are you doing here?"

Jax stood in front of her, wearing an undershirt and cargo shorts. Water dripped from his hair, speckling the fabric.

"Helen called me."

"Figures. Come on in."

The black and white dog didn't stand up, but his tail thumped on the floor.

"That's Flip."

Ivy crouched and held out her hand, palm up. He made a study of it with his nose. Flip continued his investigation, and she stole a glance at Jax. His eyes were puffy and his skin was grey. Stubble littered his cheeks.

"You look awful. Did you sleep at all?"

"Not really. Free."

The dog stood up and busily sniffed at Ivy's shoes and pant legs.

She shifted her weight. "I'm really sorry to hear about Murphy."

"Thanks." Jax looked down at himself. "I just got out of the shower, and I need to run back upstairs for a sec. Just... make yourself at home." He gestured toward the sofa. "Be right back."

Ivy sat on the couch and patted Flip while she waited. The room was spartan and tidy. She had the feeling it was less meticulously tended and more ruthlessly scrubbed. It made her think of sale houses staged for viewing, all personal photos and effects hidden away. It was unusual. But she had the impending trip to the hospital for her brain to gnaw on, and it couldn't work on two problems at once.

Jax returned, fixing the collar of his blue polo shirt. His damp hair had been combed back, out of his face.

"Can I offer you anything to drink?"

Ivy rose and moved to meet him.

"No. I'm good."

His eyes were dark with pain.

It made her heart ache. "Are you okay? Is there anything I can do?"

He held her gaze, as if he was considering her offer very carefully. Impulsively, she stepped closer and slipped her arms around his neck. He wrapped his arms around her waist and pulled her body tight against his. She stood there and breathed in the spicy citrus of his cologne, savoring the feel of his body against hers. Even the guilt that prickled her—she should not be enjoying this so much when he was suffering—didn't make her pull away. She had her own crisis waiting for her at Ben Taub hospital and being wrapped in his arms made that seem very far away. Eventually, he released her.

Eyes closed, he rested his forehead on hers for a moment. Then he moved back and took her face in both of his hands. His eyes had softened some.

"I appreciate you coming by. I really do. Don't take this personally—it's not you. I just need to be alone."

Ivy nodded. On some level, she understood that he needed to grieve in his own way. But the rejection still hurt.

"Call me if you need anything."

He kissed her softly on the forehead. Another rejection.

"I will."

Ivy turned to leave, unshed tears stinging her eyes. She slammed the car door and then hit the accelerator a little harder than she intended, scattering gravel on the road.

I hope Jax didn't see that! Don't be such a baby, Ivy. Good grief! She fumbled in the door pocket for a napkin to blot her eyes. She couldn't show up to MawMaw's hospital room looking so pitiful, so she pulled into the first coffee shop she spotted. Ivy stopped in the ladies' room to splash cold water on her face before she ordered her drink. An extra shot of espresso should shore her up to step into the grasping arms of the Buchanan clan.

Ivy passed Chance's red truck as she prowled the parking garage, looking for a spot. She was not remotely surprised to see that he'd parked just badly enough to make the space on the driver's side of his truck unusable, except for maybe a Smart Car or a motorcycle. *Some things never change.*

She found a spot three levels up, near the elevators. She texted Janelle before she got out of the car, asking her former sister-in-law to run interference with Chance. Ivy hoped that her ex had no idea she was coming, because if he did, Janelle would be no help at all. She wasn't dishonest—she just wasn't the brightest bulb in the marquee. Then again, for all Ivy knew, Chance had put his sister up to calling in the first place. Ivy shook her head. If MawMaw was on death's door and asking to see her, she'd risk having to shove Chance out of the way to do it.

She caught a whiff of Jax's cologne, wafting up from her clothes. She remembered the feel of his arms around her and got out of the car.

Her phone chimed. It couldn't send the text message. She'd have to stand outside, away from all the concrete, and hope that Janelle could get her text inside the hospital. Ivy hadn't considered this when she'd come up with her Chance-removal plan. She re-sent the text and hoped for the best.

To kill some time and give Janelle an opportunity for getting Chance out of the way (assuming she got the text), Ivy stopped in the ladies' room. She splashed more cold water on her blotchy face and patted it dry. The eyeliner pencil in her purse had just enough crayon to fix the gaps without scraping her eyelid too badly. Ivy glanced at her watch. Hopefully, eight minutes was enough. She gave her hair a final fluff and headed toward the elevator.

The tiny ICU waiting room was stuffed with Buchanans. Some glared at Ivy as soon as she rounded the corner. Avoiding eye contact with her former relations, Ivy homed in on her ex-sister-in-law, who was playing with her phone.

"Janelle?"

"Ivy! MawMaw'll be so glad to see you. Chance and Daddy's in there now."

"I thought we had a deal." Ivy hissed as she plonked down onto the hard plastic chair next to Janelle. "You said you would get Chance out of the way for me."

"What was I s'posed to do? Tell him he cain't see his momma?" She leaned back in her seat and put one hand on her belly.

"Ivy? What you doin' here, Baby Girl?" Chance stood in the doorway with his father, grinning like a 'possum eating persimmons.

She tried to squelch her anger. "I'm here to see Maw-Maw." *Not you.*

"Nurse is in there. She'll be done soon." Papa Buchanan's gravelly voice was hardly more than a whisper.

He looked so miserable that Ivy wanted to give him a big hug and tell him everything would be all right. But she was here to see MawMaw, just this once. It was a bad idea to pick up broken attachments—it would just make everything worse when they broke again at the end of this visit. Ivy just nodded.

Usually, only two visitors at a time are allowed in the ICU, so she turned to Janelle to ask her to escort her in to see Maw-Maw. *You've put on some weight. Especially around the middle.* Then it hit her.

"Janelle, are you...?"

"Yep. Six and a half months." She grinned.

"Congratulations. You've been wanting a baby for as long as I've known you."

"Lil Hank finally said he was ready. Didn't take no time after that."

A woman in hot pink scrubs stepped into the waiting area. "Alright, Mr. Buchanan. I'm all done. You can go back in now."

"Thank you, Kelly. Chance, why don't you take Ivy into see your ma?"

Ivy's jaw clenched, but she stood up and followed her ex down the short corridor to the ICU ward. MawMaw was frail and grey against the crisp white sheets and pale blue blanket. Monitor leads crept out of her hospital gown and attached themselves to a large machine. An IV stand held up three different bags, clear and yellow fluids mingling as they dripped into the line that ended in the old lady's arm. An oxygen tube ran under her nose.

"Ivy!" she wheezed.

Ivy sat down next to the bed and took the opposite hand from the IV. "Hey, MawMaw. How are you feeling?"

"Lordy, girl, I hope somebody got the license plate of that truck."

Ivy laughed softly. That was MawMaw—always had a joke for everything, even her own near miss with death. "You're as tough as they come. You'll be back on your feet before you know it. Janelle's going to need help with that baby in a few months."

"She's over the moon, ain't she? Been a long time coming."

"Is there anything I can get for you, or do while I'm here?"

"Not unless you've got a pack of menthols in your purse."

"Now MawMaw, this is the perfect time to quit. You're going cold turkey right now—just keep it up when you get home so you can dance at your grandbaby's wedding."

"Ivy, you're such a Pollyanna. That's what I love about you." MawMaw fell into a fit of coughing and the lines that scrolled across the EKG jumped erratically. Ivy shot a look at Chance.

"MawMaw, you need the nurse?"

She shook her head over the coughing. "No, Baby. Nothing the nurse can do." MawMaw leaned back against the pillows. "Pneumonia. They say you ought to stay out of hospitals, 'cuz that's where all the sick people are."

"I don't mind braving that to come see you."

"Yeah, Baby Girl, maybe you shouldn't spend too much time here. May not be safe for you."

Ivy turned so MawMaw couldn't see and scowled at Chance. "I'm sure I'll be fine."

"Well, we still shouldn't take any chances. We wanted to wait 'til you were a little stronger, MawMaw, but we have some news, too. Ivy just found out that Chance Junior's on the way."

Chapter
Twelve

J AX LOCKED THE door after Ivy left and watched through the beveled glass as her blurred silhouette retreated down the walkway. He was glad she'd come by, but he really needed to deal with this on his own. Their relationship was too new, too fresh. There wasn't the built-up trust of a long relationship there to support his emotional state. Yet. But there was someone he could turn to.

"I thought you were off today, Jax." Sergeant Miller tucked a stray wisp of hair under her hat.

"Yeah. I just wanted to come out and see Ruby. She had a long shift at the game—just wanted to make sure she wasn't sore."

"Okay. Nobody's noticed her being off."

Jax shrugged. "It's probably just me, then."

Miller's phone started neighing. "See you later." She answered the call.

Ruby stood serenely in her stall, dozing in the square of warm sun that came in from the open window. He opened the door and handed her a peppermint. She barely opened her eyes but crunched the candy contentedly. He checked her pulse. It was fine. When he came in the door, she was usually ready to go to work. Maybe it was just a lazy Sunday afternoon for everybody.

Chapter
Thirteen

"WHAT IS WRONG with you?" Ivy snarled at Chance as soon as they got into the waiting area. "Why would you tell your mother that we're expecting a baby?"

"Yore pregnant?" Janelle asked.

"Of course not! And if I was, it certainly wouldn't be by him!" Ivy glared at Chance.

Chance grinned. "Well, you used to—"

"Not the time or place, Chance. What are you going to tell her when she gets out of the hospital? I only came this one time to see her because Janelle said she was asking for me. There is no way I'm going to keep up some charade that we're still married, much less that we're expecting a baby. No. Just no."

Ivy became aware of all the Buchanan eyes on her now and felt guilty about causing a scene.

"I hope MawMaw gets better soon." Ivy turned on her heel and strode down the corridor.

"You're commin' back to see her, right?" Chance called after her.

Ivy kept walking. She was so angry her hands shook, and tears welled in her eyes. She didn't want to give her ex the satisfaction of knowing how much he'd gotten to her. She should have just shaken her head and let it roll off her back. Everybody who knew Chance knew he was a pathological liar. It shouldn't have shocked her that he'd give his critically ill mother false hope about a grandbaby just to try to manipulate Ivy back into his clutches. She hadn't thought it was possible to despise him more than she already did, but this was a new low for him.

Ivy was so agitated that she despaired of getting her pile of homework done. While her budget didn't usually allow for such indulgences, she stopped at the first coffee shop she saw and ordered a large caramel macchiato.

The warm, sugary treat lightened her mood. What story was Chance going to come up with when no baby appeared? That was *his* problem. She had homework to do.

As she came up on the Highway 59 exit off the Loop, she took the south lane, but her mind wandered north. How was Jax doing? Losing a horse, especially one that's been a partner for so long, was hard. It doesn't matter how prepared you think you are, you aren't. That ripping away of a chunk of your heart is brutal.

When Ivy got home, she went out to the barn and pulled out the cookies. The horses came trotting up from their turnouts, eager for treats. With each tidbit she doled out and each velvety nose she kissed, she felt more relaxed. She couldn't pass Amos without putting a cookie in his grasping hands. He chattered as he snatched it and took it to his water bowl to wash it.

Ivy closed her laptop. Homework complete. It was late in the afternoon and she should probably eat lunch.

Her text chime went off.

It was Jax. "You busy later?"

Of course not! But she texted, "Horses to feed, barn chores..."

"If I come help, will you go out to dinner with me?"

"If you come help, I'll cook you dinner."

"What time?"

"6:00"

"C U then"

Ivy heard Jax's truck coming up the drive and met him outside. Flash, Twilight, and Eddie jumped up and down, wagging their whole bodies until Ivy thought they'd shake themselves apart. *Dogs are good judges of character.*

Ivy kissed Jax on the cheek and took his hand. He looked tired. She wanted to wrap him in her arms to comfort him, but she knew better. It would have to be on *his* terms. If she tried to force her way inside his personal fortress, she'd never get there.

Horses whinnied and nickered as she approached the barn. Dinner time was their favorite time of the day. Except for maybe breakfast time. Or cookie time.

"There's a halter on each gate."

Jax nodded. They didn't talk much as they brought the eager horses in from their paddocks. Ivy showed him where to put each one.

"I have to finish the mats in this stall," she said, pointing to the double stall near the office. "Dr. Mueller thinks Velvet and Styx are ready to come home."

"That's great. When are you going to get them?"

"Julie and Karen just got back from their cruise yesterday. If they're up to it, we'll get the horses tomorrow afternoon."

"If they can't make it, I'll go with you."

"I'm sure they'll be fine, but thanks for the offer."

Ivy handed him a stack of feed-filled buckets. "Start at the stall closest to us on the right-hand side."

She took the other half, pausing for a moment to admire his body as he walked down the barn aisle. *Snap out of it, girl! Don't think with your gonads.* In no time, the feeding was done. Ivy made sure Amos had plenty of water on the way out. The raccoon trilled his pleasure as she scratched his back.

Ivy locked Amos' door. "How does spaghetti, salad, and garlic bread sound? Sarah Lee left a cheesecake in the freezer. I might even have a bottle of chianti."

"Sounds perfect."

When she got to the back door, the dogs crowded around, getting underfoot and making it nearly impossible to get inside.

Jax whistled, and they all turned to look at him. Ivy opened the door, and Jax and the canine coterie followed.

"I need to make a pit stop." Ivy gestured to the sofa. "Make yourself at home."

When she emerged a few minutes later, Jax was not in the living room.

Metal rattled against metal, and then she heard a steady *chop, chop, chop*.

He stood at the counter, dicing bell peppers. An onion and two cloves of garlic were lined up next to the cutting board. A skillet glistened with olive oil.

"I thought I was cooking *you* dinner."

Jax shrugged. "No point in me sitting all by myself in the living room."

Ivy's eyes met his, and she suddenly felt guilty for feeling so happy when he was hurting. She studied the wire wine rack. "I don't have any chianti. Will a Shiraz do?"

"Sure."

She poured two glasses and handed him one. Veggies sizzled as they hit the pan. Ivy's stomach growled. She hastily got out a box of pasta and a jar of sauce and got busy filling a stockpot with water.

"Let me get that." Jax brushed her arm as he reached for the heavy pot, and it sent little electric threads shooting through her skin.

She didn't dare make eye contact, sure that her feelings would be revealed. Instead, she turned and burrowed into the freezer, looking for garlic bread. Ivy was aware that Jax probably needed something to keep him occupied, distracting him from his grief, so she didn't argue when he mostly took over dinner prep.

They had just sat down to eat when the dogs started barking at the door. Ivy went to the window and saw car lights coming down the drive.

She frowned. "I wasn't expecting anyone."

Jax came and peered over her shoulder, the heat of his body tantalizingly close.

A red truck pulled up next to Jax's and parked.

Ivy seethed. *Why is* he *here? Why now?* "That's my ex. I don't know what he thinks he's doing."

Chance and another man got out of the truck and made their way to the front porch. Twilight and Eddie placed themselves on either side of Ivy, but Flash was nowhere to be found.

Ivy opened the door. "What do you want?"

"Just wanted ta stop by and thank ya for commin' to see MawMaw at the hospital."

"I didn't do it for you. I did it for her. As you can see, we're in the middle of dinner."

"Ain't you gonna introduce us?" Chance grinned at Jax.

"No."

The other man peered through the screen into the dining nook. "Ivy, you drinkin' wine? In your condition?"

J AX studied the two men. The one who had spoken first must be the ex. He was the greasy blond from the other night, when Jax found him on the side of the road, presumably changing a tire. Had he tried to lure Ivy out to the barn with a wounded puppy? *What would have happened if I hadn't been there?*

Chance was wiry and probably strong. The other man was doughy and had a beer gut. Either could be armed. Ex was the bigger threat, though.

He looked at Ivy. "Condition?"

Ivy closed her eyes and shook her head, letting out an exasperated sigh. "I don't have any conditions."

The plump man grinned. "Well, I can unnerstand why you don't wanna tell him."

"There's nothing to tell, Bobby. I don't know what kind of nonsense Chance Buchanan has been filling your head with, but after all this time, even you should know he's full of crap. He lies to his own mother without batting an eyelash."

Bobby's brow furrowed, as if he were trying to decide whether he'd just been insulted.

A low growl rumbled from Twilight's chest. Bobby shifted back on his heels, but Chance leaned forward.

"If that vicious dog bites me, I'll report it to the sheriff and have it put down."

Ivy's jaw clenched. "I wouldn't want her to get alcohol poisoning from biting you. You said what you came to say, now go. You aren't welcome here. And if the sheriff is coming out, it's to arrest you for trespassing."

Jax had left his pistol in his truck the first time he went out with Ivy, but now that she knew he was a cop, he usually kept it at his hip, as discreetly as he could. He shifted now, making sure that the black leather of the holster that peeked out from under his untucked polo was clearly visible to the two men.

Jax locked eyes with Chance. "I'm sure, Mr. Buchanan, that with MawMaw in the hospital, you have a number of things to attend to. Now is a great time to go and take care of your business."

Even Bobby, who was a few nuggets shy of a Happy Meal, was smart enough to know when to cut his losses and leave. "C'mon, Chance. You don't wanna start nothin'. Not with your momma in the hospital. I told you 'fore we left this waddn't a good idea, no ways." He put his hand on Chance's shoulder.

Chance's eyes narrowed, and he shrugged his friend's hand off of him. "See you at the hospital tomorrow, Ivy?"

"No. I only went because Janelle begged me to. Your mother was always good to me, and I thought if she really wanted to see me...before she passed, I owed her that."

"But she thinks—"

"I know what she thinks! But that's a you problem. I'm not the one who lied to her. I'm sorry. I can't see her again."

"You would let an old lady suffer in her hospital bed 'cause it ain't convenient for you? Selfish bitch!"

"That's enough." Jax's voice was calm, but stern. "You've been asked to leave. Go."

Chance's mouth opened, but Jax cut him off. "Now."

With a sneer, Chance spat on the porch and stalked down the stairs. He slipped off the last step and plunged face-first into the crushed granite walkway. Supported by a stream of expletives, Chance pulled himself to his feet. Bobby tried to help him up, but his friend slapped his hands away.

Jax put his arm around Ivy's shoulders as they stood in the doorway, watching the red truck slide out of the gravel driveway and screech onto the pavement. She was shaking.

"You okay?"

"I will be."

He pulled her a little closer, and she responded by wrapping her arms around him and burying her head in his shoulder. She didn't sob, but he felt wetness against his skin as her tears soaked his shirt. He stroked her hair. Gradually, she stopped shivering and released him.

"I'm sorry you had to see that."

"Everybody cries sometimes."

A half-smile flashed across her lips. "I meant him. Chance."

"This isn't the first time he's done this, is it?"

"It's the first time he's come up to my door. He usually just calls or texts me. I blocked his number the day I left him, but he always borrows somebody's phone or gets a new email. Can't tell you how many of those I've blacklisted."

"Have you filed a police report?"

"For what? They aren't going to do anything."

Jax stroked her jaw with the back of his hand. "I'm calling a friend at HCSO. I want you to file a report about what happened just now, and document all the other stuff, too. It'll make it easier to get a restraining order, if you need one."

"Like Chance is going to respect a piece of paper."

"Maybe not, but if he violates it, he can be arrested. There's no bail for that—he can sit in county for a year, as long as the judge thinks he's a danger."

"If he wasn't planning on killing me before, he would definitely do it after that."

Jax swallowed. She probably wasn't wrong.

"I'm still calling Connor."

The deputy's arrival was heralded by the barking chorus of Twilight and Eddie.

Jax looked out the screen door. "You should probably put them away."

She took the excited dogs to her bedroom and shut them in. When she came out, Deputy Connor, laptop slung over her shoulder, stood in the living room.

Ivy's mouth opened and closed, then she said, "Oh. I didn't expect—"

"A female?" Connor grinned. She was tall and athletic, with close-cropped red hair. Even her bullet-proof vest didn't do much to mar her hourglass figure.

Chapter
Fifteen

*W*HY DID *I just assume Connor would be a man?* "You're right. I'm sorry."

"No apologies needed. Jax said that you've been harassed by your ex-husband. Is that what you'd like to report?"

I wouldn't like to report anything. "Yes. You probably want to sit down." Ivy gestured to the dining table. "This may take a while."

Connor set her laptop down and pulled out a chair. "Jax, would you mind making sure the perimeter is secure?"

Ivy fidgeted "Is that really necessary?"

Jax's warm hand rested on her shoulder for a moment as he headed toward the door. "I think it's a good idea."

What kind of questions is she going to ask me that she needs to send Jax outside? "Would you like some water?"

"No thank you."

Ivy got herself a glass and sat down. "Where do you want to start?"

"How about with what happened this evening?"

Ivy told her. She told Connor about the phone calls from Chance, the emails, and how he stalked her on social media.

Tappity tappity on the keyboard. Ivy's fears were reduced to letters on a screen. She had mostly found Chance's antics annoying. Before tonight. Now she felt anxiety creeping in and staining the corners of her life. What would have happened if Jax hadn't been here? *Damn that Chance Buchanan!* This was the last thing she needed.

"Since you split up with your husband—"

"Ex-husband."

"Ex-husband. Have you had sexual relations with him, or encouraged him in any way?"

"What? No! Of course not."

Ivy knew she was going to have to tell her about Maw-Maw. Truly, no good deed goes unpunished.

"There is one thing." She gave Connor all the details of her visit to MawMaw's bedside, including Janelle's cellphone number. "I had thought, since his mother might not make it through this, he'd err on the side of decency. But no. Everything is about Chance, even if it isn't."

"And you're certain you didn't explicitly extend or imply any invitations to him?"

"I made it very clear that I was not interested. Half the Buchanan clan was there—ask them. Or the ICU nurse."

Connor nodded and typed more notes. After a while, she looked up. "Is there anything else you would like to tell me? Do you have any questions?"

Yes. How well do you know Jax? "I can't think of anything right now."

The officer handed Ivy a card. *Sergeant Tabitha Connor.* "Please contact me if you have any more incidents. Don't hesitate to call 9-1-1."

"Thank you."

Sergeant Connor walked out the door. Jax didn't come back in. Ivy peeked out the curtain and saw them leaning against her patrol car, talking. *What was she telling him?* Surely, she wasn't talking about the hospital incident. Maybe Ivy should tell him. But it was so embarrassing. She was just trying to help, but that was her mistake. The visit never should have happened, and she was mad at herself for letting Janelle talk her into it.

Ivy left the window and found her glass of wine. She started loading the dishwasher, but Jax came back inside before she got all the silverware in the basket.

"Ivy. That can wait. I'll help you with it later."

She wanted to run to him and throw her arms around his neck, feeling the warm strength of his body against hers. But she might also lose control. Their relationship was so new—if she fell apart in front of him, what would he think of her?

"This won't take long." It was safer in the kitchen.

He sighed and came to her, gathering the almost full plates off the table. "I'm going to put these in the fridge, just in case we're hungry later."

Ivy nodded.

Once the dishwasher was humming away, Ivy picked up her wineglass. "You want to watch a movie or something?"

"Sure."

They settled on the couch, and the saggy middle section acted like a gravity well, sliding Ivy against Jax. He put his arm around her, and she snuggled in against him, his cologne wafting up from the heat of his body. She picked up the remote.

Ivy would tell him about the hospital visit.

Just not tonight.

Chapter
Sixteen

JAX LIKED THE way Ivy's body fit against his, like a warm, soft puzzle piece. Reminded him so much of...no. He couldn't allow himself to go there. There was already enough loss today, and he didn't need to reopen old wounds. An image of a smiling Elise, Fallon in front of her, riding Murphy across the Elysian Fields flickered across his mind. They all had angel wings, and the white feathers rippled in the breeze.

Stop.

Get your head back into real life.

He gave Ivy a subtle squeeze and breathed in the floral scent of her hair. It felt good, being here with her. She understood exactly the kind of grief he felt after losing Murphy, and he was sure she would let him handle it the way he needed to. She had so far, anyway. His pain blunted his desire, and it was a relief to just sit in front of the screen.

Jax took another sip of his wine. He preferred beer, but it still soothed and relaxed him. It was tempting to look for oblivion at the bottom of the bottle. In the end, that would only make it worse, though.

His eyes were soft-focused on the TV screen. He'd forgotten what movie they were watching. Some summer blockbuster. If he watched long enough, he'd figure it out.

Ivy shifted to look at him. "Need a top up?" She raised her wineglass.

"No, thanks. I'm good."

Ivy's text chime went off. Her phone was on the dining table. She hesitated for a moment, then got up to retrieve the device.

She made a loud tsk before she responded to the text.

Was her ex bothering her again? "What's wrong?"

"You know how I told you Julie and Karen just got back from their cruise? They both have food poisoning, and they won't be able to help me pick up Velvet and Styx at the vet tomorrow."

"I'll go with you."

"Do you mind driving? I've got the trailer, I just don't have the truck. We always use Julie's."

"Not a problem. What time you want to go?"

"I've got to finish getting the double stall ready. Maybe lunchtime?"

"I'll tell you what. I'm concerned about you being here alone tonight after what your ex pulled this evening. I can crash on your couch, help you with the mats in the morning, and then go get the horses. Does that work?"

"I'd like that."

Ivy fell asleep before the movie was over. Jax listened as her breathing deepened. He didn't mind as he didn't see that he was going to be able to sleep anytime soon, so he channel surfed for a little while.

She looked so peaceful he hated to wake her up. But he needed to go to the bathroom. He assessed his options for disentangling himself.

The dogs went ballistic.

133

Chapter
Seventeen

Ivy jerked awake. Fear shot through her when she realized there was a man next to her. *How did Chance get in here?*

No. Not Chance. Jax. She let out the breath she'd gulped in her moment of panic. Trying to shake off the sleep cobwebs, Ivy stood up, went to the window by the front door, and peeled back the edge of the curtain.

"I don't see anything. The porch light is motion activated, and it's not on. It's probably just...critters. Lot of skunks and raccoons around here."

"I'll have a look, just to be sure." Jax stretched his arms.

"I'm coming with you." *The dogs need to go out to pee, anyway.*

Jax opened his mouth, and Ivy was sure he was going to protest, but he closed it again before saying, "Alright, let's go."

Ivy retrieved a couple of flashlights from a drawer in the kitchen, then flipped on the outside lights as they went out the door, accompanied by the three blustering dogs.

They walked around the entire property but found nothing amiss. Horses nickered in the dark stables, surely hoping for an unscheduled cookie.

Jax stopped short, and Ivy crashed into him. Flash, who had been at her heels, crashed into her.

"Sorry. The stars are so bright out here. And you're barely out of town."

"Being a few miles off the freeway does have some advantages. Plus, the reservoir's just south of us."

They continued on their way back to the house. Ivy liked that Jax was the kind of guy who would stop and notice a starry sky. She smiled to herself in the dark.

When they got back on the well-lit porch, only Flash was anywhere to be seen. Ivy whistled.

"Twilight! Eddie!"

Nothing happened.

She called again.

Finally, the bushes rustled, and the two dogs bounded into view.

Fortunately for both Ivy and the wildlife, Twilight had not tangled with another skunk.

Ivy opened the front door. "Probably just a 'possum."

"Probably."

As Ivy retrieved a blanket from the linen closet and a spare pillow from her bed, it occurred to her to invite him into her bedroom. After all, they were both adults. The memory of his body against hers as they sat on the couch sent a warm shiver down her spine that lodged in her solar plexus.

But was she really ready for the next step?

She couldn't say with certainty that at least part of her reaction to Jax wasn't a response to Chance's shenanigans. There was no possibility of her getting back with her ex. She was emphatically not interested, regardless of what Chance thought. It had taken her long enough to escape that relationship in the first place. It somehow felt like a corruption of something that could be beautiful to go further with Jax while she was still fighting off the plague of Chance Buchannan. He was impulsive and unpredictable. Maybe he'd finally back off, now that there was clear proof that Ivy had moved on. But maybe he would try harder, and Ivy didn't want that to poison her budding romance with Jax. She just hoped that she wasn't moving so slowly that Jax interpreted it as disinterest.

She handed him the blanket and pillow. "Welcome to the luxury accommodations at the Stonewall Inn."

His smile was infectious, and she felt her cheeks warm.

"Yes. Well. It's getting late. See you in the morning." She popped up on her toes to plant a chaste kiss on his cheek before fleeing to her bedroom, dogs close behind her.

That went well. Ivy lay in the dark, staring at the ceiling, for a long time. She tried to at least make good use of her insomnia by making mental checklists of homework that still needed doing and things around the house that needed taking care of.

But her mind kept straying back to the two men in her life, one she wanted and one she wanted to be rid of. *Would Chance try anything crazy? Would Jax lose interest if she didn't step up to the next romantic level soon?*

She heard Flash whimpering. Sh*e's just been outside. She can't possibly need to pee again.*

Ivy got up and opened the door to the crate. The puppy cowered against the back. "Flash. Come here. It's okay."

Tail between her legs, she slunk forward to lick Ivy's hand, and she coaxed Flash out. She was trembling, so I*vy* scooped her up and held her against her chest, pulling the blanket off the bed to cover them. She leaned back against the mattress, and the puppy snuggled against her. The wooden bed frame dug into Ivy's back, and she hoped Flash would calm down soon. Twilight came and curled up against Ivy's legs on the left, and Eddie settled on the right, using her knee as a pillow.

Eventually, she drifted off to sleep and had strange and steamy dreams about Jax.

Chapter
Eighteen

J AX STARED AT the ceiling fan as it whirled soundlessly in the dark. Part of him wished Ivy hadn't put him on the couch, and part of him was glad she did. He was certainly interested in knowing her better, much, much better. She was smart, kind, pretty. The horses were definitely a bonus. He thought of the way her body felt against his...he was definitely interested.

The downside was she had a crazy ex.

Was he dangerous, or just bothersome? He didn't think she wanted to go back to Chance. But when he was in Patrol, how many domestic violence calls did he go on where the victim turned on the cops to defend their attacker?

But Ivy had left him. How long ago had she said? Two years? She probably wasn't going back to Chance Buchannan, although him reaching out to her because his mother was in the hospital was a bad sign. Possessive men who couldn't let go and move on were the kind who thought murder-suicide was a solution to all their problems.

He should have checked on Ruby again. No calls from the stables saying she was sick, but something wasn't right with her. He could feel it. She was different somehow, even if she didn't look that way.

Jax closed his eyes. He saw Murphy in his head. The old horse lay in the dirt of the aisleway, an arc gouged into the path by his restless hooves. Jax sucked in a deep breath and his eyes flew open. The loss was still too raw. He needed more time, more space before he could deal with it.

He sat up and considered going outside for a run but didn't want to set the dogs off. Jax tried thinking about something, anything, to distract himself from the pain. He made it worse by thinking of Ivy's sweet face and craving the comfort of her body.

Sleep evaded him. Jax couldn't calm the noise in his mind and relax, so he did the one thing that seemed to work for him when nothing else did. He sat up and turned on the end table lamp. Ivy's printer sat nearby on a small desk, so he took a couple of sheets of paper out of the tray and borrowed a pen from her desk caddy.

So far, his movements hadn't aroused the dogs' suspicions, but he thought it best to keep his roaming around the house to a minimum. He sat on the floor and used the coffee table as a desk.

Dear Elise,

I really miss Murphy. But more than that, he was the last link to happier times. He was my anchor, and he kept me sane in this crazy world. It hurts to let go of the dead. It feels disloyal, traitorous. But those of us left behind are still here for a reason, and we have to do the best we can until we, too, cross over.

I think-and it's hard to say this-I'm falling in love. The signs are all there: the torture of anticipation, the electricity that pulses when skin touches skin, the dizzy euphoria of a kiss... But it's more than a mere physical attraction.

It's more like an alignment of stars. Maybe that sounds pretentious, but that's how it feels.

Love,

Jax

He read over the letter, folded it into quarters, and put it in his pocket. At last, his mind stilled, and sleep took him.

The horses were noisy, neighing and nickering for their breakfasts. The nights had finally started to cool, and more than a few of the equines had a good bucking round of the paddock before settling down to graze.

Jax watched as Ivy, dwarfed by the two horses she led, one on either side, sang to them to keep them calm until she could release them into the field. He was falling for her. Of that, there was no doubt. But whether that was exhilarating or terrifying was a different question.

With two of them working, it didn't take long to finish adding stall mats and shavings to the double foaling stall.

After breakfast, they hitched up the trailer and were on the way to the vet's to pick up Velvet and Styx.

"I just texted Dr. Mueller. They'll be ready to go when we get there."

"Cool."

He wished Ivy wasn't on the other side of the truck. But sitting in the middle next to him was kind of high school, he supposed.

Ivy stared out the passenger window. The unpleasant thought occurred to Jax that Chance's appearance had reignited her feelings for her ex. He banished it, but the foul thing still lurked in the dark corners of his mind.

He drummed his thumbs on top of the steering wheel. "You okay?"

Ivy sighed. "Yeah. Just not looking forward to the vet bill. I'm lucky the clinic extends credit to the rescue. But still. I sure hope we're in the top ten for the Salt River charity contest, because I'm not sure how we're going to buy hay this winter otherwise. But we've always managed before. I'm sure we will again this year."

Jax hadn't thought about that. He felt some small amount of shame that he was relieved she was worrying about her rescue's vet bill rather than pining for her ex-husband.

The gate swung open, and gravel crunched under the truck's heavy wheels as they pulled into the clinic's driveway.

Ivy went into the office, and Jax opened up the trailer and pulled down the ramp before joining her in the lobby.

Dr. Mueller was handing Ivy some paperwork, and she looked up as Jax came in.

"I'm so sorry to hear about Murphy. Dr. Clark told me about him this morning."

"Thanks."

The vet tech led Velvet out of the barn, Styx trotting along beside her. Ivy put her things in the truck and opened the escape door of the trailer.

"She should load fine. Julie had no trouble getting her in the trailer at the feed lot."

Velvet had other ideas.

Chapter
Nineteen

VELVET HALF-REARED, her eyes rolling back and flashing white. Kelly, the vet tech, was nearly yanked off her feet.

"Whoa!" She tried to pull Velvet around, but the big mare snorted and shook her head, nearly jerking the lead line out of Kelly's hands.

Styx whinnied and pranced around his mother.

"Easy, easy," Ivy crooned. She moved in and put her hand on the mare's shoulder, keeping an eye on her large hooves.

Velvet flicked an ear in her direction and turned to assess Ivy's intentions.

"It's alright. It's alright. Don't you want to come home?" Ivy slid her hands up the mare's shoulder to her mane and started to scratch her neck underneath the long hair.

Styx tried to push Ivy out of the way, but Jax diverted him.

Now on tip toe, Ivy scratched further along Velvet's mane. She started to relax and lowered her head slightly. Styx decided to take advantage of the calm and have a quick nursing session.

Ivy started humming a lullaby her grandmother used to sing to her when she was little as she moved from scratching Velvet's mane to massaging circles along her spine. The mare's head dropped more.

Dr. Mueller cocked her head, squinting. "*All the Pretty Little Horses?*"

"Works every time."

"Nobody but you, Ivy."

Ivy gave Kelly a quick smile. "I think she's afraid to leave. She's been getting good food and been treated well. If she gets in that trailer, where's she going to end up? Could be back at the feed lot. She doesn't know."

Jax leaned against the trailer. "She told you that, did she?"

"Not...in so many words." *Did he not believe her?* "I'm just going to graze her for a couple of minutes. If she has a few minutes to calm down, maybe she'll go in."

Dr. Mueller nodded. "Let me know if you want me to give her a little Ace."

"Hopefully she doesn't need a tranq, but I'll let you know."

"She's thin, but she's still sixteen hundred pounds. You're not going to be able to wrestle her anywhere she doesn't want to go." Dr. Mueller and Kelly went back inside the clinic.

Styx finished his feed and strutted back over to Jax, who started scratching along the foal's shoulder. The baby's lips began to quiver, and he raised his head in the air, doing his best giraffe impersonation.

Ivy whispered to Velvet, "While the boys are entertaining each other, let's go over here and have a little chat."

She led the mare a short distance away. Ivy didn't want Styx to think his mother was going somewhere without him—that would only make things worse. Velvet put her nose down and clipped a few mouthfuls of grass.

Ivy stroked the horse's back and ribs. She tried to hold an image of her farm in her mind and telegraph it to Velvet.

Would it work? She had no idea. Ivy had once taken an animal communication course, and the instructor had told them that animals think in pictures, so send them a picture of what you're trying to tell them. There was no way to confirm or debunk the information the students had obtained about the animals in the course, and Ivy was never certain whether it was actual communication, or just an exercise in fantasy. But it couldn't hurt to try.

To hedge her bets, Ivy also told Velvet about the large paddocks. One of them even had a bois d'arc tree, and all the horses loved gnawing on its hard, warty 'apples.' She told the mare about each of the other horses at her place, and where they'd come from. One-eyed Silver, crippled Patty, abandoned Mingo, abused Sally and her baby Cloud, Simba the mini mule, and the ancient ones, Pickle and Reverend. She'd saved them all, and she'd save Velvet and Styx, too.

Velvet continued to eat.

"Alright. Let's try again." She clucked to the horse and raised her head with the lead.

So far, so good. They were almost to the trailer door. Ivy stepped onto the ramp. Velvet raised her head and pulled back.

"Velvet! Please."

Styx squealed and raced toward his mother. He crashed into her hind legs and bounced off, staggering to keep his balance. His front feet landed on the ramp and the sudden change in the surface startled him. He tried to buck and kick out but overbalanced and rolled into the trailer.

The ramp shook as Velvet hurried up to see to her offspring. Ivy had to scramble to get out of the way, grateful she'd removed the center divider. The foal could have gotten trapped under it with his unconventional loading style.

"Get the door!"

Jax was there in an instant, closing the door on Styx's side and fastening the butt bar behind Velvet. Ivy closed her door, and they both raised the ramp, latching it into place.

Ivy shook her head. "Never a dull moment."

Unloading went much more smoothly than the loading had. Velvet lifted her head and whinnied to the other horses as Ivy turned her toward the paddocks. Styx mimicked her, his curly baby tail raised high. Jax went with her to open the gate.

The two horses in the adjacent field—a bay and a chestnut—came trotting up to see the new arrivals.

Ivy snorted. "You wouldn't guess those two are both over thirty, would you?"

She led Velvet into the paddock, and Styx raced past her. Jax closed the gate behind them. Ivy patted the mare on the neck and took off her halter. She didn't immediately go to meet the neighbors. Instead, she stopped in front of Jax and raised her nostrils about level with his and blew in his face. She gave his cheek a gentle nudge with her lip, then arched her neck and trotted toward Pickle and Reverend.

Does she know he just lost a horse? "Looks like I've got some competition."

"Not a chance." Jax grinned.

Chapter
Twenty

JAX STOPPED TO fill up his truck and get a cold drink. A little caffeination was in order. He found himself whistling as he stood at the pump. Spending time with Ivy was just what he needed to keep his mind off the raw wound of losing Murphy. Maybe instead of just going home, he'd pick up Flip, and they'd go to the dog park.

Agility training for the border collie mix was something Jax had toyed with off and on. His schedule sometimes made it hard to be consistent with training sessions. And it wasn't like he ever planned to show the dog. But working Flip over the obstacles at the park would occupy his mind, at least for a little while. The last thing he needed was to be sitting at his house alone.

Flip was more than excited to get in the truck and go somewhere. He had a doggie door so he could go out and do his business when Jax was at work, but he was probably feeling neglected, as Jax had been away for almost twenty-four hours. The dog put his feet up on the passenger armrest and sniffed at the closed window, so Jax rolled it down a couple of inches. He wondered how Flip would get along with Ivy's dogs. Maybe they should have a playdate at the dog park to find out.

After almost two hours of agility obstacles, ball-throwing, running laps around the perimeter, and swimming in the dog-bone shaped pond, Jax was ready to come home. Flip would have been happy to stay longer. He was a perpetual motion machine.

For a treat, they stopped for a coffee and a puppy latte. Flip started whining with excitement as soon as they pulled into the drive-through.

"Keep your fur on. It'll be out in a minute."

The cup of whipped cream was gone in seconds after he gave it to Flip, but the dog licked the container the rest of the way home, just to make sure he didn't miss a single molecule of the delicacy. Puppy lattes didn't happen every day.

When they got home, Jax sat down and put his feet up, clicking through the channels with the remote. The next thing he knew, he opened his eyes and discovered it was 3:00 AM. For a moment, he thought he was at Ivy's place, then realized it was his own plaid sofa. He left the TV on for company and went back to sleep on the couch.

Jax brushed Ruby and picked her feet. She seemed to be half asleep, which was unusual for her. She was typically alert and eager to go to work. Her pulse was normal, and she didn't feel unusually warm or cold to the touch. He scratched her jaw, and she rested her head on his shoulder, eyes closed. He rubbed her cheeks and forehead. She yawned.

"Were you out partying last night, girl?"

Jax put the saddle pad across her back, then settled the saddle into place. As he drew up the girth, Ruby swished her tail and stomped one hind foot. As it tightened more, her ears flattened and her lips curled back, as if she were threatening to bite. He pulled off the tack and checked it carefully for burrs or wayward nails that had worked themselves out of the saddle. Nothing. Jax put his ear against her belly. Lots of gurgles, so she probably wasn't colicky. Next, he ran his fingers down her spine, one hand on either side, checking for soreness. She didn't react until he got almost to her hips, then she roached her back and pinned her ears again.

He put her back in the stall and went to talk to the LT.

"There's something wrong with Ruby."

"What's she doing?" Lieutenant Wilson leaned toward him, her waist-length blonde braid scrolling down her back.

"She just seems lethargic and her back is sore above her kidneys."

"The vet's coming out Tuesday. As long as she's eating and pooping, she should be fine to wait a day. I'll ask Alphonse to keep track of that. Ballinger's on vacation, so why don't you work Sam today?"

Sam was the size of a tank—a Clydesdale x Percheron draft horse mix whose breadth strained the hips. Jax liked the personality of the benevolent behemoth, but Sam wasn't his favorite horse to ride.

"Alright. I'll get him tacked up."

Sam snoozed in the cross ties while Jax brushed what seemed like two square miles of him. The massive horse didn't resist picking up his nearly dinner plate-sized hooves to be cleaned, but he didn't exactly help, either. Jax worked up a sweat just getting Sam groomed. The horse yawned and took a deep breath when Jax started tightening the girth.

"Really? We're going to play that?"

He bridled the horse and led him toward the mounting block. He stopped a few feet away to finish tightening the girth, now that the horse had exhaled the extra air he'd sucked in. Sam didn't even seem to mind that his nefarious plot had been foiled.

The other officers were already in the arena warming up. Today, they would be practicing working in pairs and negotiating a few obstacles. More than once, he wished for agile, responsive Ruby. Most of the time, he only needed to think what he wanted her to do, and it was done. Sam took several seconds to respond, but then again, he was almost twice her size, and that was a lot of bulk to change directions. And that's what made him one of the best crowd control horses. Nobody was going to keep standing in his way once he started moving in their direction. It would be like facing down a Mack truck.

After the training session, and Sam was back in his turnout paddock, Jax felt like a cartoon bow-legged cowboy. Officer Tim Balliger, who normally rode him, was a former NFL linebacker who was 6 feet 4 inches of solid muscle and wider than most doorways, didn't seem to have that problem. For both their sakes, he hoped nothing was seriously wrong with Ruby.

The vet was late. When he finally arrived, Ruby was last on his patient list. Jax struggled to keep himself from trying to hurry Dr. Clark along.

Finally. It was her turn.

Dr. Clark took her respiration and temperature, felt along her spine, and looked in her mouth. Then he asked his assistant to get some OB gloves out of the truck. When she came back, he pulled one up all the way to his shoulder. Jax winced as the doctor's arm disappeared into Ruby's posterior. He made a few faces during the short palpation.

He pulled his arm out and stripped off the glove. "Your mare's pregnant."

Chapter
Twenty-One

❧⚹❧

IVY HAD BROUGHT Velvet and Styx into the round pen. She had no idea what kind of training Velvet had, if any. A surprising number of horses ended up in the kill pen because they had never been trained properly. Or at all. The halter that had been on Velvet when Ivy had rescued her from the kill pen was still on her head. She didn't object too strongly to having a lead snapped on or off but wouldn't let anyone near her ears.

Styx made his shrill foal whinny and trotted around the perimeter. Ivy used her phone to video his silliness for a few minutes before she turned her attention to his mother. Velvet wasn't tied as Ivy brushed her. The mare enjoyed her grooming from the shoulders back, but when Ivy tried to work her way up Velvet's neck to the horse's poll, she yanked her head straight up in the air and pinned her ears.

Ivy sighed. "We'll work on that."

If she couldn't be bridled, she probably couldn't be ridden. Maybe Jax could help out with her this weekend. Ivy didn't want to overdo if she was out here by herself. Who'd call 9-1-1 if she got splattered across the fence?

She knew she should probably ask Julie, her partner in the rescue, but she and Karen were still weak and recovering from food poisoning. Besides, Julie had been adamantly opposed to Ivy buying Velvet, and Ivy wanted to have some progress to show before Julie came out and gave her another lecture.

There was no denying that Julie and Karen both would fall head over heels for Velvet's foal.

Styx paused his prancing to investigate the rubber curry mitt. Ivy stroked his nose and part of his neck. His lips quivered. The staff at the vet clinic had been good about handling him every day, even after Velvet was able to nurse him and he no longer needed bottle-feeding. He would be easy to train. His mother was the question mark.

Ivy went into the tack room and retrieved a container of cookies, the soft molasses and oat kind that most horses found irresistible. She broke one in half, then offered one piece to Velvet and one to Styx. Velvet's ears pricked forward, and she raised her head. But she didn't move toward Ivy. Styx imitated his mother.

"Come on, don't you want a cookie?" Ivy gave a little whistle. Every horse within earshot looked up.

The mare took a step in her direction. Styx couldn't help himself. He trotted up and shoved his muzzle into Ivy's hand, nearly knocking the treat into the dirt. She had watched him nibble at grass and stick his head into his mom's feed bucket, but he hadn't quite gotten the hang of eating solid food yet. He grabbed the sweet nugget with his lips and trotted off, shaking his head, until he dropped it in the grass. While Ivy was laughing at his antics, she felt warm breath on her other palm. She turned her head just enough to see Velvet gingerly taking the cookie. Once it was swallowed, the mare fixed Ivy with her blue eye.

"Of course you can have another one." *Sometimes a little bribery gets the job done.*

Ivy retrieved a few more cookies, and by the time it was all said and done, Styx had mastered gumming the soft treat and swallowing it. Velvet was hooked, and Ivy was her new best friend, or at least her dealer, at any rate.

Ivy held the treats low, around knee level. When Velvet was comfortable standing close to Ivy with her head down, she would gradually start trying to touch the mare's head. Hopefully, it wouldn't take too long for the horse to learn to trust her, but she also knew that sometimes abused animals never did regain their trust in humans. She couldn't blame them, really.

She put the pair away, then brought in the other horses and fed them. Amos chattered at her, waving a forearm through the cage at her, begging for one of the horse cookies from the container near his enclosure.

"You're a raccoon, not a horse. Can't you read?" she shook the container gently at him as she handed over the treat.

Ivy sighed as she trudged back to the house. She had a ton of homework, and she had to get on social media and beg people to vote for the Copper Penny Rescue for the charity contest. She'd been slacking on that and needed to pick up the pace. If her rescue wasn't one of the winners, she wasn't sure how she was going to buy hay for the rest of the winter. Julie did have a point that saving Velvet was going to be very expensive, and it didn't make economic sense to spend the money on what may well have been a lost cause. But if horse rescues only did things that made economic sense, there wouldn't be any horse rescues.

Now she had some video of an adorable foal trotting around. If that didn't inspire people to vote for Copper Penny, she wasn't sure what would.

Chapter
Twenty-Two

❧⸻❧

"WHAT?" Lieutenant Wilson almost shouted. "There must be some mistake. There's no way Ruby could be pregnant."

Jax chewed his lip. "Actually..."

"What do you mean, 'actually'?" Her hands rested resolutely on her hips, above her duty belt.

"You remember that workshop we went to last month? And the stallion from down the road that broke out and came to visit? He let a lot of the horses out of their stalls. I didn't think Ruby had been...exposed."

The LT rubbed her forehead. "Okay, Doc. Would you check Cinder as well?"

Jax ran his hand along the top of Ruby's neck, smoothing her mane. "What are we going to do with you?"

"That's an excellent question." Wilson pursed her lips and shook her head. "I only have one other horse in training, and he's nowhere near ready for prime time. You have four, maybe five months before she needs to go on maternity leave. And if Cinder's also in foal..." She shook her head and exhaled loudly.

Jax untied Ruby and led her out of the stanchion. When he got to her paddock, he dug a peppermint out of his pocket and unwrapped it for her. She chewed it, eyes half-closed, then wandered over to her water bucket for a drink.

When he returned to the barn, Cinder, a dapple grey Percheron cross, stood placidly in the stanchion. Dr. Clark stripped the shoulder length glove off his arm. "Congratulations, I guess."

Lieutenant Wilson raised her hands in exasperation. "How can this even happen? They're both on hormones—they aren't supposed to be able to get pregnant."

"Well, sometimes that can make their cycles irregular when you take them off for the fall, and you might get a transitional estrus you weren't expecting. Especially if there's a stallion around."

Wilson shook her head. "Fantastic. If I have to sojourn two officers to Traffic, I'll probably never get them back."

Traffic? Jax tried to keep his face expressionless, but he frowned inwardly. If he couldn't do Mounted, he'd rather go back to Patrol. If he didn't want to write tickets or direct traffic all day, there was only one thing he could do.

Jax had to find another horse.

Chapter
Twenty-Three

❧❦

JUST one more day. Ivy only had to make it through Friday. And then it would be the weekend. Jax had promised to come out on Saturday to help with Velvet. Ivy felt she'd made some progress toward curing the head-shy mare. Not cured enough to take the halter off, but she could at least use the curry mitt on Velvet's face now, as long as she didn't try to go above the horse's eyes. That happened when horses got eared down a lot. They were afraid of a human pulling and twisting on their ears and hurting them.

Work seemed to take about 27 hours to get through. Why did Ferdinand keep adding more pieces to each project, just when she thought she was finished? He wasn't even the department head—Vern was, but while the other managers took care of their own stuff, Ferdinand seemed to think he should get special treatment.

"Oh. I need to add these eight slides to the PowerPoint for the meeting in the morning. Is it really 5:45 already? Hadn't noticed. Sorry."

"I know you already made twenty copies of the budget projections for the meeting that starts in five minutes, but I made some changes. Can you reprint them?"

"No, I don't know how to work the new calendar software. That's not really my job, anyway. Can't you just handle my calendar?"

Ivy couldn't tell if he did it out of spite or extreme disorganization. Come spring, it wouldn't be her problem anymore. Vern had promised a promotion and substantial raise once she got this degree she'd been working so hard on. It would move her up two pay grades to Business Analyst. She'd still be working with Ferdinand, but in a very different capacity. And with a pay upgrade. That would give her a little more breathing space, and she might even be able to have more than $4.12 in her emergency fund.

That's what kept her going when it sometimes seemed too much.

As soon as Ivy got home, she changed clothes and went out to the horses, the dogs following along, certain they'd be needed in at least an advisory capacity.

It had been a long day, and leaving late put her in the worst of the traffic, so it took an additional half hour to get home. But it was Friday evening, and Jax would be out tomorrow. She found herself humming as she brought the horses inside to have their dinner. Amos seemed quite surprised when she picked him up and gave him a little spin as if they were on the dance floor. He regarded her as if he thought she might be losing her mind as he retreated into his box with the cookie she gave him.

"Silly raccoon." Ivy didn't think she'd ever smiled so much while cleaning out Amos' enclosure.

Darkness had crept up from the east, and the brilliant orange and pink sunset had bleached to grey by the time Ivy returned to the house. She cleaned up and put a frozen meal in the microwave.

While she was tidying up the barn after the horses' breakfasts, Ivy heard tires crunching in the gravel driveway and looked up to see Jax's truck.

Don't run to him. Desperation's not a good look.

She stopped raking the aisleway to smile and wave at Jax. The dogs were much less circumspect and raced to greet him. He kneeled to pet all three of them and was nearly bowled over by a canine frenzy of affection.

Twilight and Eddie had never done that with Chance. They were clearly smarter than she was about people.

Ivy scooped the last bit of wayward hay into a half-empty tub of manure and leaned the rake against the wall as he approached.

"Hey, Jax."

He leaned in and kissed her on the cheek. "Hey."

She felt her lips turning into a smile of their own volition. "Glad you could make it." She linked her arm in his and started leading him toward the tack room. "The vet said that Velvet could start on light work, but I don't even know if she's ever been ridden or anything. She is a bit head shy. Not sure we can get a bridle on her just yet—I don't even know if I have one that will fit her - but I would like to try a saddle and see what she thinks."

Jax nodded, his eyes on the swirling pool of dogs that flowed around them as they walked. "If she's rideable, what's your plan? Velvet's a nice-looking mare. You going to sell her?"

"Don't know. Haven't got that far yet. I've been focusing on trying to get her healthy, and I usually end up finding homes for the healthy ones. Their adoption fees help keep the unrideable ones in grain. But I'm kind of attached to her. Way too early to decide."

Jax nodded absently. "I see."

Ivy pointed to the racks. "Can you grab the saddle with the plaid cover and bring it out to the cross ties? I'll go get Miss Velvet."

"Sure."

Ivy grabbed a few cookies and left the tack room. When she got to Velvet's paddock, she whistled. The horses on either side came trotting up to their gates, and she gave each of them one of the sweet tidbits.

Velvet had been trotting around the paddock, tail raised, since Jax's truck had arrived. She stopped and gave the vehicle a hard look before she turned toward Ivy. Styx whinnied and started jogging toward the gate. When Velvet broke into a canter, Ivy felt the earth shaking underneath each thunderous stride the huge horse took. Styx, not to be outdone, stretched out his neck and galloped, reaching the gate first, but swerving away and circling back because he hadn't planned his stop in time. Ivy snapped the lead line onto Velvet's halter and gave each of them a treat.

Back at the barn, she clipped the mare into the cross ties and removed the lead. Velvet stood quietly while Ivy brushed her. Styx decided now was a good time to nurse, and that kept him out of trouble for a few minutes.

"Can you pick up her feet?" Jax asked.

"Yeah. You have to lean on her to get her to pick them up, but she will give them to you."

He stroked the horse's neck and ran his fingers through her mane. She yawned. "She seems to be settling in."

Ivy peered around Velvet's rump as she brushed the mare's hindquarters. "Yes. She's getting better about having her head touched, but I think she's having a hard time trusting that she's safe now. Every time a truck pulls into the driveway, she gets antsy."

"Is there a hoof pick in that tack box? I'll do her feet."

"Sure. There's one in there somewhere—it'll be in the top shelf thing. I usually wait until I'm putting the horse away to do the hoof treatments."

Ivy liked that Jax was being so helpful. She could really get used to that. And it didn't hurt that he was easy on the eyes. Keeping busy probably kept him from dwelling on Murphy. She retrieved a mane comb from the trunk and started working on Velvet's tail, watching as Jax leaned into the mare while squeezing on the tendons along the back of her leg. He clucked to her, and she lifted her big hoof. She didn't hold it up for him, but she did let him handle it. Styx walked through the open stall door and laid down to have a nap.

A saddle pad. How'd I forget that? Ivy went into the tack room to find one.

When Jax had finished picking Velvet's feet, Ivy held up the saddle pad. "You ready?"

"Ready as I'm going to get."

Ivy held out the square pad so Velvet could see it. Then she let the mare smell it. Ivy rubbed the pad along Velvet's neck and shoulder before settling it on her back. So far, so good. She repeated the process with the saddle. No negative reactions. So far. She attached the girth on the off side, and Jax pushed it toward her so she didn't have to lean under the mare's belly. She buckled it so that it touched Velvet's skin, but wasn't snug.

Velvet stomped one hind foot.

Fly or girth? Let's find out.

She pulled on the first billet strap and snugged up the girth. Not quite tight enough for a rider, but almost. Velvet's ears flicked backward, but she didn't do anything else.

Jax scratched underneath the mare's mane. "Good girl."

Ivy tightened the girth another hole. Velvet grunted, but didn't offer any resistance.

"Okay. Let's take her out in the round pen and see what happens."

Once in the pen, Ivy led her around the circumference twice, then unclipped the lead line. Velvet put her head down and nibbled the grass that grew along the outer edges of the railing.

Jax laughed. "Whoa there, girl. Calm down." He reached between the rails and scratched Velvet's haunch.

Ivy leaned against the railing. "Looks like she's done this before."

"You want me to get on her?"

"You sure? Just because she's tolerating the saddle doesn't mean she'll take a rider."

"I know that, but I have a hunch she'll be fine."

The sparkle in his eyes made Ivy smile. "I think Julie's helmet will probably fit you. It's the mint green one in the tack box."

"I'll be fine."

Ivy crossed her arms. "No helmet, no ride."

Jax tried to scowl at her but couldn't keep a straight face.

A few minutes later, he returned wearing the helmet. Velvet snorted at him and reached her nose out to sniff the strange thing that now clung to his head. Deciding it wasn't dangerous, she resumed grazing.

Ivy snapped on the lead line and carefully repositioned the saddle and tightened the girth before taking the mare to the center of the pen where a mounting block stood. Jax climbed on top of it slowly, talking to Velvet the whole time. He leaned his weight against her. No reaction. He lay across the saddle. She shifted her feet to accommodate the extra weight. Carefully, he swung his leg over her back and sat upright. The mare glanced back at him.

Ivy stroked Velvet's shoulder. "Ready?"

"Let's go."

Ivy led Velvet around the pen. She didn't seem the least bit bothered about Jax sitting astride her back.

"I think she's been ridden before. She feels pretty balanced."

"Good to know," Ivy said over her shoulder.

A piercing whinny came from inside the barn. Styx must have woken and not seen his mother.

Velvet whinnied back, her whole body shuddering so violently that Jax had trouble keeping his seat.

Styx screamed again.

Velvet jerked the lead out of Ivy's hands and took two galloping strides toward the barn.

She's going through the fence!

Velvet leaped like a deer over the round pen railing. All of that momentum launched Jax out of the saddle, and he hit the ground with a thud as the mare raced to the barn.

Chapter
Twenty-Four

———❧———

Tʜᴇ sᴡɪꜰᴛʟʏ ᴀᴘᴘʀᴏᴀᴄʜɪɴɢ ground walloped the oxygen right out of Jax's chest and he gasped for breath. He saw stars for a moment.

"Jax!" Ivy was on her knees beside him. "Are you okay?"

He nodded, air starting to seep back into his lungs. Ivy helped him sit up. He still couldn't talk, but he rapped his knuckles on the helmet and gave her a thumbs up.

"Are you sure you're okay? That was quite a fall—you were probably twelve feet in the air or more."

"Fine," he gasped. He knew it was a long fall. He'd looked down at the horse's head, neck, and back after she'd launched him out of the saddle.

Still panting, he got to his feet and let Ivy lead him toward the barn.

He sat on the tack trunk and watched Ivy unsaddle Velvet and put her away. He took off the helmet and set it next to his thigh.

"Come on in the house. I'll get you a glass of iced tea or something."

Jax sank onto the couch. Ivy pulled his boots off and put his feet on the coffee table. He'd had a broken rib before. There were no hot, stabbing pains when he moved, so he didn't think there were any fractures. But between the heaving for breath and the high-speed collision with the earth, he'd likely be sore tomorrow. He'd take some ibuprofen before bed and first thing in the morning, and it would be okay.

Ivy returned with a huge tumbler of iced tea. "Is there anything I can get you? Ice pack?"

"I'm fine. Really."

She looked skeptical. "I'm glad you had a helmet."

"Me, too. I'd like to ride Velvet again, though. We, uh, got off to a bad start."

"Well, not this afternoon. Maybe tomorrow. I'll have to keep an eye on her to make sure she didn't injure herself. She clearly failed to read the vet's note that said 'light work.'"

Jax let a smile slip over his lips. "For the few minutes I was on her, she felt really good. And she's very athletic."

"Clearly." Ivy smoothed his hair. "I want you to just relax for a while, so I can make sure you don't have a concussion." She studied his eyes.

"I'm fine. Really." He took a slug of tea. *Is now a good time to tell Ivy about Ruby? Maybe not quite yet.* "What's on Netflix?"

He allowed Ivy to fuss over him for a while. But his pride was more injured than his body, and he started to feel a bit too mothered. He leaned forward and stretched.

"I've got a ton of stuff to get done, so I need to hit the road."

"Are you sure you're okay?"

"Yes." He leaned in and kissed her quickly on the lips. "I'm happy to come out tomorrow, if you need more help with Velvet."

There was a flash of something in her eyes that might have been disappointment. Yeah, that might have come out sounding like he was more interested in the horse than her. "Or if you just want to have dinner..."

"Let's play it by ear, huh? I've got a project to finish, and we'll have to see how Velvet's doing tomorrow. I should probably go check on her now, actually."

He followed her out to the barn and leaned against a support beam as Ivy looked in on the mare. She pulled Velvet's lip back and pressed a finger against her gums, looked in her eyes, and checked the horse's pulse.

And looked damn good doing it.

"What do you think?"

"She seems fine." Ivy passed him on the way to the office.

A gentle hand caressed Jax's right butt cheek. *Somebody's feeling frisky.* His laundry could wait a little longer.

Warmth flowed down into his lower body, and any soreness in his ribs melted away. He turned to pull Ivy into a kiss. Confused, he found himself alone in the barn aisle. "What the...?"

Car keys jingled as they thudded into the dirt at his feet. The pole he'd been leaning on was a corner of the raccoon's enclosure.

"Amos! Knock it off." Jax snatched the wad of keys before the grasping paw could pull them into the pen. Amos chattered at him.

Little perv.

"Did you say something?" Ivy closed the office door behind her.

I got groped by a trash panda. "Just talking to Amos."

"I knew you'd get to be friends." Ivy took his arm.

Not that kind of friends. Jax grunted noncommittally.

Ivy walked him back to his truck. He cupped her cheek in one hand and kissed her softly. "Call you tomorrow."

"Sounds good."

She stood in the driveway, and he watched her shrink in the rearview mirror as he motored down the caliche.

Sunday afternoon was cool and cloudy. Breezes flicked a few dead leaves off drowsy trees and swept them up into short-lived whirlwinds before scattering them on the grass. Jax's back was a little stiff from his fall the day before, but it was mostly fine.

Styx alternately trotted and grazed around the outside of the round pen. As long as Velvet could see him, she was calm. Jax had taken the lead line from Ivy after she'd led Velvet around the round pen a few times. Just by shifting his weight, he could get her to move out or slow down. If he closed his thighs and stiffened his lower back, she drifted into a lazy halt. Squeezing his calves against her pushed her into a slow jog. He didn't have to tug on her head at all.

Velvet came to an abrupt stop and raised her head, ears pricked forward. A plastic bag cartwheeled by on the wind. Ivy chased after it.

Was Velvet a good candidate for police horse school? Could be a win-win for both he and Ivy. If she would allow the mare to be evaluated, and the horse passed, he could pay the adoption fee himself and donate Velvet to the Mounted Patrol program. Ivy'd get the money for her rescue, and he'd have a horse to work with while Ruby was on maternity leave. Styx, of course, would stay with his mom until it was time for him to be weaned. Or would they be a package deal?

And it might bring him and Ivy closer. If he could bring himself to allow it.

Jax slid off Velvet's back. She was on light work, after all. The mare still hadn't gained all the weight she needed, although she looked a whole lot better than the first time he'd seen her. He stroked her neck. "You're a good girl, Velvet."

She nickered to Styx.

Jax led her into the barn and put her in the cross ties. *Where's Ivy?* He found himself whistling as he brushed Velvet. Styx trotted into the grooming stall and began to nurse urgently, as if he'd been kept from his dam all day. Jax knew it hadn't been forty-five minutes since they'd brought the pair of them in from turn out.

He scratched the foal's butt, and Styx swished his tail. *Not a bad-looking baby.* Twilight and Eddie capered into the barn aisle. Velvet pinned her ears at them and stretched her muzzle in their direction. The dogs scampered off.

Now Jax was starting to get concerned. *Where was Ivy?*

Chapter
Twenty-Five
❧

I VY MUTTERED UNDER her breath as she chased the plastic bag. Some helpful yaupons caught it for her, though, their almost-ripe berries shining orange in the cloud-filtered light. A mockingbird scolded her from the uppermost branches.

"Those berries are all yours," she replied to the bird.

Barking. Her head whipped toward the sound. Twilight and Eddie appeared to have something cornered in a clump of bushes about thirty yards away. She went to investigate. It wouldn't be the first time they'd discovered a dumped kitten or injured wildlife.

"Eddie! Twilight! What have you found?" she called as she made her way in their direction.

A yelp from the shrubbery made Ivy's feet move faster.

"Eddie, get out of the way." She pushed the Pyrenees mix with her knee.

Their alert duty completed, he and Twilight trotted off together. Ivy kneeled and peered into the bush. There was Flash, looking as pitiful as a wet cat, collar caught on the rusty remains of a long-removed barbed wire fence.

"Poor pup!"

Flash whined in response.

Ivy unbuckled Flash's collar, and she almost knocked Ivy over, jumping up to lick her face.

"Okay, okay. Calm down." Ivy scooped the puppy into her arms. Flash was growing faster than she was filling out, so she was still thinner than she ought to be, but she was probably up to fifteen pounds, maybe twenty. Her tail beat back and forth, an unsteady metronome.

When they got to a more open area, Ivy set Flash down and put her collar on. She looked up with mournful eyes, and Ivy picked her up again.

"You're getting too heavy to tote around." But she carried the dog to the barn.

Jax leaned around Velvet's neck. "There you are."

"Flash got stuck in the bushes." She set the puppy down, but the dog just sat on her feet.

Velvet stretched her neck up and twitched her lips as Jax scrubbed between her front legs with the rubber curry mitt. Styx supervised from the aisle.

"She really seems to like you."

"She's a good mare." Jax straightened up and looked at Ivy over Velvet's back. "So, just out of curiosity, if someone wanted to adopt her from your rescue, what would the adoption fee be?"

Ivy cocked her head. She'd never get back the money she'd put into Velvet's hospital bills. No one would spend that much money on a rescue horse, because being abused or neglected stigmatized them in a way 'normal' horses were not. Although it was true that many needed physical and/or mental rehabilitation before they went on to normal and productive lives. "I'm not sure. I hadn't given it too much thought yet. Do you know somebody who's interested?" She gave him a half smile.

"Besides me?"

Ivy raised an eyebrow.

Jax's face turned serious. "I really think she might be a good police horse. I'd like to adopt her and have her evaluated. If she doesn't pass, I'd keep her as my own personal horse. And Styx, too, of course."

"Oh." Ivy hadn't seen this coming.

"Our horses are treated better than we are."

Ivy opened her mouth, then closed it again. "I'm sure they are. Let me talk to Julie and let you know tomorrow."

Chapter
Twenty-Six

JAX HAD PLANNED on doing yardwork when he got home from Ivy's place, but by the time he'd gassed up his truck and made a surgical strike at the grocery store, it was already getting dark. Instead, he sat on his back deck with a hot cup of decaf.

What on Earth am I doing? I've ridden Velvet for all of twenty minutes and am already trying to make a police horse out of her. He watched Flip trot around the back yard, investigating each and every scent trail left behind by the large population of fox squirrels. His black fur faded into the twilight until it looked as though disembodied white patches zig-zagged across the grass.

Jax sipped his coffee, chuckling at Flip's antics, but his thoughts returned to Ivy and Velvet. Was turning Velvet into a police horse a good idea? Was he just trying to replace Murphy? Maybe it didn't matter. The Copper Penny Rescue needed the money, and Mounted needed more equine cadets. In a few years, Styx might even join.

A sudden burst of music made him jump. He answered the phone, "Hey, Ivy."

"Hey. I've been talking with Julie. We both agree that Mounted would be a great place for Velvet, if she passes evaluation, of course. If for any reason you can't take care of her, she comes back to the rescue. Her adoption fee is $1,500."

Jax knew that was probably about a tenth of her vet bills. "Is that going to be enough?"

"She's going to need extra farrier work because her feet aren't in great shape, and a lot of TLC to overcome the abuse. No way of knowing how extensive it was. Maybe it was only at the feedlot, but she was pretty skinny when we found her, so she was starved at some point."

"Understood. I'll need some time to make the arrangements. Can I pick her up next weekend?" He kept his voice even, though he was more excited than he probably should be. Velvet might wash out, and he'd be back in a patrol car with a radar gun.

"Sure. Whenever you want."

"You can come with me, see her new digs. Then maybe we could go out for dinner or something."

"Sounds great."

He hung up and chugged the rest of his lukewarm coffee.

Adopting that mare was one of the craziest things he'd ever done. So was risking his heart.

Jax dropped into a chair in Lieutenant Wilson's office.

She didn't look up from the stack of paperwork in front of her. "What is it, Carter?"

"I think I've found a horse."

"In a stable? Congratulations."

"To be evaluated for the program."

Wilson looked up. "I see."

He could tell he'd piqued her interest, even if she did little to show it.

"Big paint mare. Draft cross. Does have a foal that's still a few months off being weaned, though."

"Yeah, well, we've got a regular maternity ward going as it is, so she'll fit right in. When can you bring her?"

"I was going to pick her up over the weekend."

Wilson looked back down at her paperwork and picked up her pen. "I'll need three copies of her Coggins and health cert."

The week dragged by, but Saturday finally dawned, and Jax arrived at Ivy's early enough to help put the horses out. Velvet and Styx trotted around the paddock, enjoying the crisp air before settling in to graze.

Ivy stared after them for a long minute.

Jax turned to her. "You can come see them any time you want. They'll have top care."

"I know. It's just...nothing. Let's go take care of the paperwork."

Inside, Ivy opened a manila envelope and pulled out several sheets of paper. "Here's the original and three copies of the Coggins and health certificate that you asked for." She set a stack of papers on the table. "Here's the adoption agreement. I need you to sign and date it." She handed him a pen.

Jax read through it, signed his name, and handed over the check he'd filled out earlier. *No going back now.*

"Okay then. Let's get your horses loaded up."

Velvet was not eager to get into the trailer, but once Styx was inside, she walked right in. Jax and Ivy got in the truck and pulled out of the drive. Ivy stared out her window.

"You okay?" Jax reached across and stroked her hand

"Yeah. I've just gotten attached to those two. Velvet is a really special horse, and I hope you realize that."

"That's why I adopted her. You can come visit any time."

"I know. I keep telling myself that they're going to a great home, and now there's a slot for another horse that needs help."

"But you'll still miss them."

"Yes."

He patted her hand again. He wanted to hold her, to tell her how he'd love to take care of her, too. But he couldn't say the words. "So how's school going?"

Jax listened to her talk about nearly-impossible-to-please professors, end of semester papers, and parking space short-ages. He asked questions here and there to keep her talking, because he just liked the sound of her voice.

It seemed like almost no time before they pulled up at the police stables. Ivy's eyes widened, and he wondered what she'd expected.

Lieutenant Wilson came out to watch them unload. She inspected both horses, then Jax handed her the paperwork, and she went back inside.

Ivy hugged Velvet and scratched under her mane. Styx demanded his own attention, which Ivy indulgently provided. She was slow to leave the horses and get back into Jax's truck.

Rigatoni was one of Ivy's favorite restaurants, and sort of on the way back to her house. After horsing around all day, they certainly weren't dressed for fine dining. Rigatoni was fast casual, so they'd fit in with the regular clientele, even if they were perhaps more aromatic.

After the drinks were brought and food was ordered, Jax took a big swig of his iced tea. "So, Thanksgiving's coming up. You traveling to visit family?"

Ivy blinked twice. "No. Someone has to take care of all the critters. Got some local cousins, may hang out with them some. How about you?"

"My sister always has a feast going on. It's so over the top, it's ridiculous. You would have to see it to believe it."

A shy smile crept over Ivy's lips. "Are you inviting me to Thanksgiving?"

"Would you like to come?"

"How could I miss such a spectacle?"

There was a battered white truck in Ivy's driveway when they pulled in. Her face fell. "What does he want?" she muttered.

The truck door opened and the doughy man that had shown up with Ivy's ex-husband a few weeks ago got out.

Ivy threw open her door and lunged out, slamming it behind her. "Bobby, why are you here?" she growled at him.

He grinned a gap-toothed grin. "Now that you're in a family way, Beth Ann thought we oughtta get you somethin'."

Chapter
Twenty-Seven

*W*HAT? Jax did a double take at the package that the chunky man held, sloppily wrapped in pastel baby shower paper.

Ivy looked like she was about to spit nails. "Bobby, what the hell? Seriously. Why are you here? With that stuff?"

The big man looked confused. "Chance said—"

"How long have you known Chance? If his lips are moving, he's lying. I am not now, nor have I ever been in a family way." Ivy put her arm around Jax's waist and snuggled aggressively against him. "And if I was, it certainly wouldn't be with Chance Buchanan. I thought that was clear after your last unwelcome visit."

What have I stepped in the middle of? Second time this has come up. Is there something Ivy's not telling me? Jax shifted his weight to keep his balance with Ivy pressing hard against him.

Bobby wilted like hot spinach.

Ivy sighed and moved slightly away from Jax. "Bobby, why don't you take that to Janelle? She actually needs baby stuff."

He tossed the lopsided package into his truck and turned to look dejectedly at Ivy.

"Bobby, please go. I appreciate that you're trying to be nice. Thank you. But has listening to Chance ever gotten you anything but trouble? Think about that on your way home."

"Goodbye, Ivy." He shot Jax an angry glance before slamming his truck door and revving the engine.

Jax watched the dented pickup shimmy and rattle its way out of the driveway. When the single working taillight disappeared around the shrubby corner, he turned to Ivy. "What was that about?"

She shook her head. "It's a long story, but the executive summary is that Chance's mom had a stroke, forgot the last two years of her life, and he tried to cheer her up by telling her that he and I were expecting a baby."

"I see."

Jax cast his eyes to the road, checking to see that the truck hadn't stopped on the road. How far would this guy go to try to keep his hands on Ivy? "Does your ex own a gun?"

"Several."

"You might want to consider that restraining order we talked about last time he showed up."

"You're probably right. But when am I going to have time to do that? And even if I did, it wouldn't stop him."

Her voice had an edge, and he wasn't sure whether she was annoyed with him or scared. He squeezed her shoulder and ran his hand down to the small of her back. "Do you want me to stay?"

She stretched up and kissed him, quickly, on the lips. "I wish. But I'm so far behind on my homework, I'm going to be up half the night as it is. I'll take a rain check, though."

"If either one of them comes back, call 9-1-1."

"I will."

"And then call me." He folded her into his arms and gave her a long, slow kiss. He felt her body relax against him, while his started to tense up. If he was going to go, he'd better do it now.

"You call me if you need anything. Anything at all."

"I will." A smile flickered around her lips.

He watched her walk up the steps and unlock the front door before he got into his truck.

The Mounted stables weren't exactly on his way to the house, but he wanted to see how Velvet and Styx were settling in before he went home.

Jax found himself humming over the radio as he navigated the sluggish freeway traffic. His shirt smelled of Ivy's light perfume, and he could still feel the warmth of her body. He craved more...and yet he held back. So far, he'd convinced himself that he was just being a gentleman. But was 'just being a gentleman' code for 'too scared to get close because another loss would kill him?' He turned up the volume on the radio and sang louder to drown out any further thoughts.

When he arrived at the stables, Alphonse was just starting to bring the horses in from their turnouts. Velvet raised her head and gazed warily at him. He didn't see Styx.

Where is he? Hurrying over to the paddock, he found the baby lying flat on his side. Jax ducked between the metal rails of the enclosure and Velvet snorted at him.

Styx sat up, groggily shaking his head. He'd been napping.

"Hey, you wanna grab your horse?" Alphonse called to him from the edge of the barn aisle.

"Sure." Jax picked up the lead line that hung on the gatepost and clipped it onto Velvet's halter.

Styx trotted along, whickering, as Jax led them to their stall. Jax ran his hand along the foal's back as he jogged by. "Nice-looking boy. You did good, Velvet. Now, let's get you into the Police Horse Academy, huh?"

Two weeks passed Jax by like a bullet train. He spoke with Ivy every day, and she came out on the weekends to see Velvet and Styx. And him, of course. It felt like she just belonged. Belonged with him. Belonged in his life. And it scared him a little. But not enough to put any distance between them.

He was a little distracted, thinking about her, while he was working Velvet. Jess McClintock, the trainer was out, and they were doing an exercise where the horses had to walk through thick smoke while people made all kinds of noise around them. He should never have let his attention drift, but Velvet had been so calm.

One of the volunteers loomed out of the billowing fog with his arms raised, and fast as a snake, Velvet bit him on the arm. It was a warning—she didn't break the skin, and she could have broken bones—but he yelled out. The instructor came running. The stunned volunteer was led away for first aid.

Lieutenant Wilson shook her head. "Put her away for now."

Jax slid down from the mare's back and led her to the crossties to untack her. "Velvet, why did you do that?"

He'd worked with her every day and gotten her to not only put her head down to be haltered or bridled, but to let him massage her ears. And now? The LT might just kick her out of the program.

Velvet was washed and put away and Jax led Styx up and down the barn aisle. He felt eyes on him and looked up to see Wilson leaning against the tack room door, watching him. Jax closed the distance and stopped. Styx stamped his front hoof impatiently.

Wilson reached out and scratched the colt's neck. "That was bad."

"I know."

"No one is likely to care if she bites a purse snatcher, but if she bites someone's kid...that's a lawsuit, and maybe euthanasia."

"I know. It was at least partially my fault. Got too relaxed with her."

The lieutenant nodded slightly and pursed her lips. "She's been nearly perfect at everything else. I'd hate for her to drop out of the program, but I can't have her biting civilians, either. I think we should have McClintock work with her individually for the next week or two and see if it can be fixed."

Jax nodded. "I agree." At least Velvet was getting a second chance. He'd gotten quite attached to her. True, she would still be his personal horse if she failed out of police horse school, but that left him with no replacement for Ruby when she went on maternity leave.

"You look tense." Ivy's brow furrowed. It was too warm in the restaurant, and she wished she had a fan.

Jax took a sip of iced tea, then explained Velvet's precarious situation.

Ivy, sitting next to him in the booth, reached for his hand, and he intertwined his fingers with hers. "She can always come back to the rescue."

"I know." He fiddled with the silverware packet. "Here's the thing, though. You remember me telling you about when we went to that conference, and a stallion from a farm down the road came and let a bunch of horses out?"

Ivy cocked her head. "Yes."

"It turns out that Ruby and another mare, Cinder, got bred."

Her eyes widened. "I see how that could be a problem."

"There was one horse in training, now Velvet makes two. If they fall out of the program, Officer Sanchez and I are getting seconded to Traffic."

"Grilled cheese?" A different waitress from the one who had taken their order stood at their table, a plate in each hand.

Ivy raised her tea. "That's mine."

The server nodded and set the platters down in front of them. "Enjoy your meal."

Jax rearranged his fries. "I like what I do. If I was going to move to any other department, it would probably be Homicide."

"You'll feel better if you eat something. Velvet has gotten a second chance. Sounds like Lieutenant Wilson really likes her. That mare is whip-smart. I think she'll be able to figure it out."

"I hope you're right." Jax dragged a fry through the ketchup on his plate. "Speaking of eating, are you ready for Thanksgiving?"

Chapter
Twenty-Eight

———✦———

BUTTERFLIES flapped in Ivy's stomach, and she wasn't sure she'd be able to eat anything. Jax was on the way to pick her up to have Thanksgiving dinner with his family. He'd worked the parade earlier in the day, but they had a little time to spend together before they were off to his sister's River Oaks home.

Ivy had little occasion to visit the ultra-swanky side of town, and she worried that there would be unwritten rich-people rules that everyone would know but her, and she'd look like a fool.

Ivy couldn't focus long enough to do any schoolwork, and she couldn't sit still long enough to watch TV.

Am I going to make a good impression?

What if they don't like me?

To try to keep her anxiety at bay, she started on a much-needed tidy-up.

May as well vacuum the dog hair off the couch.

When she pulled the cushions off to get at the dreaded under-cushion ecosystem, a folded piece of paper fluttered to the floor.

"What's that? Probably lecture notes or something."

She picked it up and unfolded the page. Jax's handwriting scrawled across the paper.

Dear Elise:

I hadn't believed it before. Time passes. Things change. New people come into your life and suddenly, the world is different. It's been a long time since I felt this way. I needed to tell you. I hope you don't think I'm being impulsive. It seems...disloyal. And yet, the sky looks bluer, the stars seem brighter, and I feel more alive than I've been in years. I know I should tell Ivy everything, but it just never seems like the right time. I'll come out to New Haven and see you soon.

Love,

Jax

Ivy swallowed hard. Who was this Elise person? Had Jax been making plans to see her while he was staying over at Ivy's? She felt like someone had hit her in the gut with a baseball bat. All the air in the room was sucked out. Blinking back tears, she got a drink of water. Her hands shook so much, some of it spilled and splattered on the floor. She read the letter again. And again.

She'd thought Jax was different. But he was just as bad as Chance Buchanan, maybe even worse, since he'd seemed like such a genuinely good guy.

Her cheeks were tear-stained and her eyes were puffy when his truck pulled up. Her head throbbed, and she did not get up to let him in. He came up on the porch and knocked on the door.

The dogs ran to greet him, tails wagging.

Traitors.

Ivy stood, reeling between anger and sadness.

As soon as he saw her face, his mouth fell open. "Ivy? What's happened?"

She swallowed hard. "How are things in New Haven?"

His eyebrows knitted together. "Why are you asking about New Haven? I don't understand...."

Ivy opened the screen door and handed him the note.

Jax glanced at it and his face fell. "I can explain."

"I'm sure you can. But I don't want to hear it."

"Ivy. Wait."

She teetered on the knife's edge. It would be easy to fall into his arms. But she remembered how many chances she'd given her ex. "Goodbye, Jax."

Chapter
Twenty-Nine

❧

JAX STOOD BLINKING at the closed door. *What the hell just happened?* One minute, they were on the way to Thanksgiving dinner at Helen's house, and now they were apparently finished.

He raised his hand to knock. If she'd just open the door, let him explain...*What's the point? She clearly doesn't trust me enough to even talk about it.* He'd have to think of another way. There had to be another way. Jax shook his head and strode back to his truck, threw the letter on the seat and slammed the door.

I suppose I should have told her. It's not like it's a huge secret. I could have said, "Oh, by the way, my wife and daughter died in a car wreck because I failed to see the other car barreling through the intersection." Jax breathed a bitter sigh and scrubbed at his eye with the heel of his hand. *I should have been paying closer attention. But it was raining so hard, visibility was terrible. I should have pulled over and waited for the rain to let up. Or been more vigilant. I was the driver. I was responsible for their safety.*

If he sat still enough, he could still feel the warmth of Elise's body as she lay dying in his arms, her bright blood soaking his clothes. No matter how hard he tried, there was nothing Jax could do to stop it. Too much damage. So much adrenaline pumped through his body that he didn't feel his dislocated shoulder until much later. Right now, he wanted to vomit.

"Ajax! Darling." Helen stood sparkling in a metallic gold sweater in her foyer. "Where's your girlfriend?"

"She isn't coming. And no, I don't want to talk about it."

His sister rubbed his arm. "Okay. Come on in. Virgie says the turkey will be done in another half hour."

There was nothing Jax wanted less than Thanksgiving dinner. But what choice did he have? He'd never hear the end of it if he ghosted the family function. Besides, how many more holidays did their dad have left? He'd gone into a decline after their mother passed last year.

And Jax had to admit that while he craved solitude, it was probably the worst possible thing for him right now.

Jax got himself a glass of water and joined the gathering, a fake smile plastered across his face. Dad was in the recliner, dozing off over the newspaper. Helen and Morgan's kids, Francesca and Morgan Jr., were wearing outfits that probably cost more than his truck, and they looked bored to tears, sandwiched between their parents on the oversized, elegant, and very expensive couch. There were about a dozen aunts, uncles, and cousins he saw once or twice a year, and some of Morgan's family that he barely remembered. They were a bit snobby and standoffish, and he hadn't made much effort to reach out to them.

Except for Irene. Morgan's mother was that quintessential sassy old lady who spoke her mind and didn't care what anybody thought. While some people called her blunt (among other things), he thought she was honest. Just not tactful. But who has time for tact at ninety-eight?

He'd just lost Murphy (has it been three weeks already?) and now Ivy had left him. If he were home alone, he'd just brood and get himself in an even more wretched state. He knew Irene would talk for hours if he got her started. He made his way around the room, offering a "hello, good to see you" here and a handshake there.

Jax had just about made it to Irene's chair when Helen tapped a wineglass with a spoon. "Virgie says the food is ready!"

As everyone filed into the cavernous formal dining room, Helen went to wake Dad. He grumbled a little but got out of the recliner. Jax grabbed the handles of Irene's chair, as Morgan had left her to manage on her own and wheeled her to the table.

"Thank you, hun." Her voice was thin and reedy.

"Of course, Irene. How've you been?"

"Falling apart, but here I am. Much to Morgan's chagrin, I'm sure." She glanced up at her son, who had already seated himself at the head of the table.

"That can't be true."

"Ha." Her eyes twinkled, and she reached up and pulled Jax by his collar so his face was closer to hers, and she whispered in his ear. "It's a secret. Don't you dare tell anyone. They don't know I changed my will. Donating almost everything to charity. My attorney has already set it all up. They'll challenge it, I'm sure. But they'll lose. They already have enough money. I want mine to go to someone who actually needs it. In fact, I've already started doling out some grants."

Jax chuckled. "I like the way you think."

Morgan's sister, Cordelia, eyed Jax suspiciously from across the room, then went back to her conversation with someone from her side of the family that he didn't know. Everyone else had found their seats, and the four children sat sullenly at the kids' table in the corner.

Jax sat next to Irene. "What kinds of organizations are you supporting?" He expected her to name a big foundation or two; maybe the Alley or the Houston Ballet.

"Eh, a little bit of everything. Just gave $10,000 to Casa de las Madres. They provide baby supplies–diapers and formula and whatnot–to women who can't afford them."

A young lady in a grey uniform dress with a white apron set bowls of mushroom seafood stew in front of them. Another poured white wine into a glass at each setting.

Jax picked up his spoon. A mini octopus tentacle curled out from under a stalk of asparagus. His stomach churned.

Irene used a fork to pick out the solid bits in her bowl. There were no baby cephalopods in her portion, he noticed. *Wanna trade?* The tiny tentacled arms reaching out of the bowl had already put him off the soup, but he felt obligated to eat at least some of it. He pulled a slice of portobello out of the broth and put it in his mouth.

It was reluctant to go down, so he spent the rest of his time moving things in the bowl around with his spoon and talking to Irene.

Soon the soup course was whisked away and what he assumed was a salad was set in front of him. Translucent slices of cucumber were somehow fashioned into a bowl, which corralled chopped greenery and parmesan slices. Endive antennae sprouted above the greens, and one ultra-thin slice each of beet, carrot (lengthwise), and bell pepper formed an abstract sculpture in the center, punctuated by florets of broccoli.

Irene snorted. "Have you ever seen anything so ridiculous?

"No. No, I haven't." Jax ate the vegetable slices, and some of the parmesan before that course, too, was remanded to the kitchen. He had no idea what to expect for the appetizer.

The two young ladies brought out aggressively yellow plates with a cylinder of congealed vegetable salad topped with a thick slice of partially cooked egg. A triangle of seeded toast jutted at a jaunty angle from a dollop of what he guessed was salmon mousse, balancing precariously on one corner.

"That's different." Irene speculatively poked the aspic with her fork.

"Not exactly what I expected at Thanksgiving dinner. But I'm sure it's nice."

"I'm sure it's very expensive and tasteful. Not sure about tasty, though.

Jax tried to conceal his laugh with a cough. Helen gave him a look and raised an eyebrow.

Irene nudged his elbow. "I think we're being naughty. We'll be at the kids' table if we don't watch out."

"Or out on the curb."

"Oh, no. The neighbors might see, and Morgan would be mortified." She sighed. "It's not his fault, I suppose. His life has just been one flat plateau. No adversity to overcome, no tough decisions to make. I tried to persuade his father to either send him to the military or the Peace Corps, but he wouldn't hear of it. I love him–he's my son." She gave her half-raw egg a forlorn glance. "But he is very shallow. How can you appreciate the mountains if you haven't been in the valleys?"

"Valleys are overrated."

"Oh, honey, I know you've been in some tough places." She patted his hand. "Are you doing okay? You do look a little peaked."

"I'm okay."

"You sure? You need a lady friend. That would do you a world of good."

"Maybe."

"Faint heart never won fair maid."

"Ah!" Hellen chirped. "It's the turkey–the *pièce de résistance*."

The grey-clad women set Wedgewood blue willow china plates before each diner. In the middle of each plate, four turkey breast medallions leaned on a pile of green peas which were trapped by a smear of sauce that may or may not have been mustard. A two-inch square of mystery baked good (dressing?) lay off one corner. Diagonally across from it, three slices of sweet potato were topped with pecans and drizzled with white sauce.

Irene blinked at the plate, then cocked her head to one side. "What the hell is this?"

Morgan gave his mother a condescending smile. "It's turkey, Mother."

"I think you mean this meal is a turkey. I wish you'd just ordered from Luby's." Irene blotted her lips and stood up. "In fact, I think I'll just go there."

Morgan smirked. "You don't drive anymore, Mother."

"I don't need to. Jax here will take me."

Jax nearly choked on the sweet potato he was chewing.

"Come on. Let's go."

Jax took a gulp of his tea and got to his feet. "If you'll excuse me?"

———— ⚲ ————

Irene clutched his elbow and practically dragged him out the front door. He helped her into his truck then checked his phone for the closest cafeteria.

Irene put her fork down, a third of a fat wedge of pumpkin pie still on her plate. "That really hit the spot. Thanks for driving."

Jax chuckled. "Did I have a choice?"

"Yes. But you wanted to get out of there just as much as I did."

She wasn't wrong.

"We were talking before your sister served up that pretentious pablum. You look more down in the dumps than I think I've ever seen you."

"Well, you know my horse, Murphy died recently."

"Yes. And I'm sure you're very sad about that. Anybody would be. But there's more to it than that. I can feel it."

Before he could stop himself, he spilled his guts about Ivy.

When he was finished. Irene nodded. "I thought it must be something like that. So what are you going to do about it?"

"What can I do? I don't want to turn into some crazy stalker. She said she didn't want to see me anymore."

"Boy, I didn't say you should act like a fool. You still have some charity gala business left, right? You don't even have to talk to her. Just show her what she's missing out on. Let her come to you, if you want her back."

Jax wanted her back more than anything he'd wanted in a very long time.

Chapter
Thirty

A COLD, LONELY WEEK dragged by.

Ivy threw herself into her schoolwork and final social media push for the charity awards. Ten thousand dollars would guarantee winter hay and pay down a good chunk of Velvet's medical bills.

How are they doing? So many times, she'd picked up her phone to call Jax. But she couldn't.

She missed him more than she thought possible. When Chance had cheated on her, and it was probably the first time he got caught, rather than the first time it happened, it was the last straw. The final insult. She kicked him to the curb and didn't look back.

But Jax. Oh, Jax, why? I thought you were different. I thought I could trust you. I thought...never mind. There's no point in pining over things that can never be.

Her ringtone startled her out of her miserable reverie.

"Hey, Julie."

"We are picking you up on Saturday, right?"

"I haven't been feeling all that well. I may just skip it."

"No, Ivy. Unless you are in the hospital or dead, you are not 'just skipping' the awards banquet. Take some DayQuil and slip on that ball gown. We'll be there at six."

"Fine."

Ivy ended the call and sighed. Jax would almost certainly be there. Would he bring his new girlfriend? Ivy tortured herself, imagining what she would look like. Long blond curls brushing her tiny waist? A dark china doll bob and sea-green eyes?

"Just stop." Ivy rose and got herself a glass of water. She had to stop this. He might not bring his new girlfriend. He may not even come. Of course, he was going to come. She would just avoid him. No problem.

There was no hiding the dark circles under her eyes, even in the poor reflection on the microwave door. She'd have to remember to pick up more concealer on the way home from work tomorrow.

After she drained her glass, she slipped on her shoes and went out for a final check on the horses. The dogs went with her, clowning and cavorting, but never straying too far.

Ivy paused at Velvet and Styx's empty stall. She missed them almost as much as she missed Jax. But that was the whole point of rescue, wasn't it? Save 'em, patch 'em up, and re-home 'em. Rinse and repeat. Each one that found a forever home opened a slot for the next broken soul in need.

But sometimes, it still sucked.

Silver's muzzle poked through the bars of his stall door, and Ivy paused to give him a smooch.

"You're with me until the end, aren't you? Nobody appreciates a blind horse, but I think you're amazing."

The horses were contentedly munching hay. But Amos complained at her until she relented and gave him a cookie. He trilled what she liked to think was a 'thank you,' and trundled off to his hammock.

Back in the house, Ivy brushed her teeth and put on her nightshirt. It would have been a great time to try to work ahead on school stuff, but it was almost the end of the day at almost the end of the week, and her brain had turned to oatmeal. She clicked through the local channels a few times before she finally settled on a rerun of 'Charlie's Angels.' She was asleep on the couch before the Angels finished getting their assignment.

She should have been happier—it was Friday morning, after all. But gloom had sunk like a cannonball into the pit of her stomach. She dreaded going to the banquet alone tomorrow. Okay, technically, she'd be there with Julie and Karen, but the original plan was to go with Jax. She'd spent her lunch hours all Thanksgiving week shopping for the perfect dress or at least one that looked good and didn't break the bank.

A whinny shook Ivy out of her stupor. Breakfast was late.

Ivy was slipping her cell phone into her purse to leave for work when she got the text from Helen. Why was she texting? Hadn't Jax told her they weren't together anymore?

There was no message, just a picture.

It was one of those old-fashioned wrought iron arches, the kind on gates to Victorian mansions in the movies. It had lettering on it.

New Haven

Blood rushed to Ivy's cheeks. *What is Helen trying to say? She's going to shove Jax's other girlfriend in my face?*

Her hands were shaking so hard she had trouble seeing the next picture that Helen sent.

It was a polished black gravestone. C A R T E R dominated the top. Two names—Elise and Fallon—were carved beneath a weeping angel. Ivy blinked rapidly. What had Jax's note said? *Dear Elise...I'll come up to New Haven and see you soon...*

She plopped into the driver's seat of her car and buried her face in her hands. *Oh. My. God. How could I have gotten this so wrong? This is probably the worst mistake of my life, and I doubt I can fix it. I've ruined everything.*

She replied to Helen. "Thanks. I didn't know."

It was then that she noticed the born/died dates. They had both died on the same day, and Fallon was only two. A tear slid down her cheek. *How awful. No wonder he didn't want to talk about it.*

Somehow, Ivy managed to get through the day at work, even though she was sorely distracted by Helen's text. *Should I message Jax? Has he already blocked my number? Maybe I should just try to talk to him tomorrow. Face to face.*

200

I look like something the cat dragged in. Ivy frowned at her reflection as she dried her hair. She hadn't slept well, and dark circles underlined her eyes. Her face was blotchy and her hair uncooperative. Julie and Karen were supposed to arrive in forty-five minutes to pick her up, but knowing Julie, it was likely to be closer to thirty.

She got to work with concealer and foundation, and by the time she finished her eye makeup, she looked presentable. She slipped into her dress but couldn't get the zipper all the way up by herself. Help would be knocking on the front door any minute now. She was putting on her earrings when the dogs started barking.

Karen knocked on the door, and Ivy let her in, trying to keep the excited dogs from bowling her over.

"Wow! Red really suits you." Karen patted Twilight's head.

"Thanks. Would you mind zipping me up?"

Karen pulled the zipper the rest of the way while Ivy put in the second earring. Then she slipped on her shoes and they got in the car.

They were about halfway to the hotel when Julie said, "You're awfully quiet back there. Everything okay?"

Ivy hesitated. "No. You know that letter I told you about? The one Jax wrote to someone named Elise?"

"Yeah."

"Well, it turns out she's dead. I'm not sure who she was—a wife, a sister, or something else. But she also had a baby that died with her. I just accused him of cheating and didn't even give him a chance to explain. He's never going to speak to me again."

"He had opportunities to tell you. He does know why you and Chance broke up, right?"

Ivy shrugged. "I suppose."

When they pulled up in the parking lot, Ivy spotted Jax's truck. Butterflies in her stomach flapped so hard they almost made it up into her throat. How was she going to get through this?

Chapter
Thirty-One

JAX WAS TALKING to Helen when Ivy and her two friends came in. Caught between anger and desire, he fell silent.

Helen glanced over her shoulder, then smiled at her brother. "You should go talk to her."

"She was pretty clear. She's not interested."

A bald man in a tux beckoned to Helen, and she sighed before leaving Jax. "André, darling. What can I help you with now?"

Jax's eyes lingered on Ivy in her figure-hugging red gown. Jealousy flashed through him as he noticed other men doing the same. But she wasn't his anymore. Maybe she never was. He decided to see if Helen needed any help.

She didn't. But he avoided the rest of the mix-and-mingle part of the banquet just the same. Finally, he heard the sound of a spoon on a wineglass, and Helen announced that it was time to be seated. As the Decorations Committee Chairman, he sat up on the stage with the head honchos. It made him feel awkward, but less awkward than sitting at the Decorating Committee table with Ivy.

As the smartly dressed hotel staff began distributing the meals, Helen introduced the first speaker. "Ladies and gentlemen, thank you for being a vital part of the Houston nonprofit community and coming here tonight for our charity awards banquet. Please extend a warm welcome to Vice

President of Public Affairs of our contest sponsor, the Salt River Group, Mr. André Boisseau."

The crowd applauded as he made his way to the podium. All Jax heard was a baritone blah, blah, blah. He got caught looking at Ivy. She held his glance for several seconds before she looked away. She looked distressed. Was it because of him? He turned sideways in his chair, so that it would be harder to look at her.

A waiter set a plate of salad in front of him, while another set down baskets of rolls. He ate the tomato wedge and the croutons. Eventually, the staff whisked away the salad plates and replaced them with the entrée. For a large crowd meal, it looked pretty good. Not as good as Ivy, though. He reached for a roll and glanced at where she was sitting. She was looking at him.

Their eyes locked. Seconds passed. Too long to stare, but not long enough to connect. Ivy dropped her head and pushed lettuce around her salad plate.

André finished speaking, and someone else started. Jax paid no attention until the person next to him stood up.

"...and finally, the chair of the Decorations Committee, Ajax Carter."

Caught daydreaming, he bolted out of his seat. The crowd applauded politely. He wished he was at home. He glanced at Ivy. At least she was clapping for him.

Helen rose and motioned for the committee head to be seated. "And now, what you've all been waiting for—the winners! Please welcome to the podium our celebrity presenters—the queen of charity galas, Mrs. Anna St. Germain, and the amazing quarterback of the Houston Texans, who gives so much back to the community, Capricorn Collins!"

The audience rose to its feet, thunderously applauding as the elegant Mrs. St. Germain glided across the stage from the left, and the towering Mr. Collins strode in from the right. His bowtie matched her sparkling aqua gown, and they greeted each other with air kisses.

Helen uncovered a table to the left of the dais, and acrylic trophies glittered under the stage lights. "Winners, when your name is called, please come up on the left side of the stage. Once you've received your award, move to the right. We'll be taking photos afterwards, and you will have an opportunity to get your picture with our presenters. With no further ado, let's get started."

Jax hadn't been one of the first six winners, but he plastered on a smile and clapped for them.

"Number seven..." Anastasia purred.

"Is Bookstar! Ajax Carter, come on up!" boomed Capricorn.

What?

Jax scrambled to his feet and walked awkwardly around the podium to receive his trophy and a large manila envelope with "Bookstar—Ajax Carter" printed on it.

He wanted more than anything for Ivy's Copper Penny horse rescue to get called. He knew how much she needed the money. Plus, if she was waiting onstage with him for photos, maybe they could talk. But eighth and ninth places went to other charities. *Still one more chance...*

"And now, the number one most upvoted charity. The winner is..." crooned Anastasia.

"Lovin' Bowlfuls! Katherine Edgemont!" Capricorn all but yelled.

Jax liked Katherine. She'd done a great job on the decorating committee. But he wished it had been Ivy. His eyes fell on the spot she'd been sitting. She was already gone. Jax sighed. He should be a whole lot happier about winning $10,000 for his charity. He had lost his chance to explain and win her back.

Sunday morning should have been a day to sleep in. But he had to be at work in the afternoon for the football game and he had a lot to do before then. He couldn't stop thinking about Ivy in that red dress. *She kept looking at him—was she having second thoughts?*

As much as he wanted her back, the last thing he wanted was to be the stalkery ex, like her former husband. But the way she'd held his eyes during the banquet.... Was it just wishful thinking on his part, or was she interested in talking?

There was only one way to find out.

He blotted his wet hands on the dish towel after he finished cleaning and refilling Flip's water bowl. Instead of picking up his phone, he knocked it right into the sparkling pool of dog water.

He swore as he yanked it out and dried it off. *Don't turn it on. Don't turn it on.* He grabbed an unopened bag out of the pantry. *Does it matter if it's brown rice?* Jax poured it into a bowl and buried the phone. He still had his old one, SIM card still installed, from when he upgraded six months ago. He'd kept the line, because he got free Netflix if he had a plan with at least two lines, even though he rarely used that number. *Was it even charged?*

Jax dug the device out of the drawer and plugged in the USB. He could call while it was charging.

Here goes nothing. He dialed Ivy's number from memory.

Chapter
Thirty-Two

‎I‎VY SAT IN the corner of Silver's stall. She breathed in the sweet scent of fresh hay. It was for her what chicken soup is to other people. But now it reminded her of the times Jax had helped her feed the horses, and the comfort had a sting in its tail.

Silver nuzzled at her hair from time to time, and she reached up to caress his velvety nose.

"At least you don't think I'm the world's biggest loser."

His breath was warm on her cheek.

"I've just screwed everything up. I drove Jax away, and he's one of the best things that's happened to me in a long time. I wanted to apologize to him, but Julie started getting sick again and we had to go before the banquet was over. We didn't even win any of the grant money. I should have spent more time promoting it, I guess. But between you guys, and work, and school—I have to sleep at some point. We'll just do what we've always done, I guess. We'll get by somehow."

Ivy sighed and Silver lazily flicked an ear. His eye was half-closed.

"Are you falling asleep?"

She kept her hand on his cheek as she got up so she didn't startle him. She didn't know how he had lost his eye—that's how she found him, standing in the same feed lot where she'd rescued Velvet, terrified and skinny. His head had drooped almost to the ground, and he seemed to have given up on life. She couldn't not take him.

"Fine. You have a nap. I've got stuff to do, anyway."

Amos' enclosure needed cleaning. Fortunately, raccoons preferred to bury their waste, so he had a big litter box where he did all his business. Ivy gave him two cookies to keep him occupied while she was scooping. She didn't need his close, personal supervision.

Ivy was changing out the raccoon's water when her phone rang. She didn't recognize the number. At least half the time, unknown numbers were Chance calling her from someone else's phone. *Talking to Chance Buchanan is the last thing I need right now.* She let it ring.

"They can leave a message," she informed a disinterested Amos.

She looked at the dusty interactive dog toy on the floor and guilt washed over her. She hadn't put treats in the puzzle for him in far too long. *Poor Amos. I think I have some grapes.*

"I'll be right back."

The dogs followed her to the house, cavorting and zigzagging as they chased each other. Inside, each one got a rawhide treat to keep them occupied while she studied. Finals were next week. One semester down, one to go. She quickly cleaned up Amos' toy and filled it with grapes—much better for him than cookies—and took it out to him. It started drizzling on her on the way back to the house, so she broke into a jog.

She put on the kettle for some hot tea and opened her notebook. *Where to start?*

It didn't really matter. Ivy couldn't focus on her studies, anyway. Her mind kept drifting back to Jax and how handsome he'd looked at the awards dinner last night. He'd kept looking at her. Maybe... *If only I'd had the chance to talk to him.* She looked at her phone. Her open textbook lay in front of her, and she tried to force herself to look at the highlighted text. Ivy picked up her phone, swallowed hard, and put it down again. She repeated this ritual half a dozen times before she worked up the nerve to call him.

It went straight to voice mail. *At least he hasn't blocked my number.* "Hey, Jax. Um...call me...when you get a chance. I was...um...wondering how Velvet and Styx were doing. Bye."

Now, she had no more excuses to avoid the books.

She looked at her phone for a long minute. *Call me back. Please?*

Chapter
Thirty-Three

MONDAY MORNING WAS clear and chilly. Jax was glad of his steaming hot coffee as he sat in his chair during roll call.

Lieutenant Wilson shuffled some papers at her podium. "Good morning, people. The Mayor's got visiting dignitaries for a trade relations meeting, so we'll be out in force around City Hall. Assignments as noted." She gestured to the whiteboard behind her. "There's a BOLO for a white or Hispanic male, about five-foot-eight, with shoulder-length hair, large scar on his forehead. Wanted in connection with a shooting on the east side."

"Jess is going to be out next week to teach some new skills to our ponies. That'll be on a Tuesday, then we're going to train with SRG on Thursday night. That's all I've got. Be safe. Test your Tasers."

After the buzzing and popping had stopped, Wilson said, "Hey, Jax! Come up here for a minute."

He took a sip of his coffee and made his way over to her. She didn't wait for him to speak.

"I know Velvet's not ready for regular patrol, but there have been reports of some suspicious characters, cabin break-ins, and one attempted robbery up at the city park at Lake Houston. We've been asked to patrol there, see what we can turn up. All the other horses are going to be at the mayor's trade meeting—we're short-hoofed. It's going to be you, me, and Tim. And Jess is going to meet us up there with her own horse. It is part of Velvet's training. I'd like to see how she goes when she's away from home. And besides, this will be, quite literally, a walk in the park."

"What about Styx? Velvet may...react to leaving him behind."

"He's big enough to be without her for a few hours. Alphonse'll keep an eye on him and make sure he doesn't get into any trouble. She may get a little upset, but they'll both be fine."

Jax had a bad feeling about this assignment. *What if Velvet refused to get on the trailer? Nobody was going to be able to force 1800 lbs of 'Nope!'. What if she was so worried about leaving her baby that something went wrong, either on the trailer or in the park?* He'd never felt so much resistance to an assignment before. But whether he liked it or not, he had a job to do.

"I'll get packed up."

Velvet had whinnied for Styx most of the way to Lake Houston. Aside from shaking the entire trailer, everything was fine.

The air was so different from the city as they unloaded the horses under the towering loblolly pines at the park. It was cooler, fresher, and the breeze in the pine needles sounded like the ocean.

Velvet was fidgety when tied to the trailer. Jax rubbed her forehead before he started saddling her. "I know girl. Styx is fine. We'll be home soon. Don't worry."

The mare raised her head, turning her body against the trailer and snorting as she stared into the woods.

Through the trees, the park manager's white truck crept along toward the trailers. It stopped well away from the horses, and two men got out, wearing khaki uniform shirts. One was tall and lanky, with an unruly shock of white hair. The younger, shorter man was doughy around the middle and had a full beard.

The white-haired man called out as he approached. "Glad y'all could make it. I'm Clark Tatum, the supervisor. And this is my right-hand man, Stanley Bouton."

The LT gave her horse a pat on the shoulder and moved to intercept the men. "I'm Lieutenant Wilson." She shook both their hands. "Can you give us about five minutes to finish tacking up, then brief us on what we're looking for?"

"Sure."

As soon as the horses were ready to go, the officers gathered around the two park managers.

Clark unfolded a map. "We're here." He traced his finger along one of the roads to a campsite. "There are some cabins along here that people have reported having their things taken from. There's been some men seen in the woods, but nobody's got close enough to get a good description."

Jax briefly raised his hand. "How many men?"

"Between one and three."

"Are there any campers here now?" Tim Ballanger asked.

Clark turned to Stanley. "How many we got? Half a dozen?"

"Eight. There's a family of four and two couples. Family's in one of the lake cabins, and both couples are over here." He leaned over Clark and pointed to the farthest campsite on the map from their current location.

Wilson nodded. "Go mount up." She stayed to talk to Clark and Stanley for another minute or two while the other officers got on their horses. She sprang onto her chestnut gelding and motioned the group forward. "Let's ride."

After an hour's worth of patrolling, they saw plenty of birds, squirrels, and a deer. But no potential thieves.

Wilson stopped her horse. "We're going to take the next left—that'll take us on the back side of the lake, and we'll be headed toward the trailers."

Jax gave Velvet a little scratch along her mane. *You've done a great job. Didn't even spook at the deer.*

She stamped a hind foot. *Poor girl. Your bag is full, isn't it?*

They started up again and made the turn. Coming towards them, a young woman pushed an all-terrain stroller along the hardpack trail. As they got closer, Jax noticed a young toddler asleep inside it. A child a year or two older walked a few yards ahead, stopping every two feet or so to pick up little things at the edge of the path.

"Liam!" the woman called when the horses got close. "Come here!"

The child reluctantly went to her, and she scooped him up.

"Good morning." Wilson smiled at the boy and gave him a little wave.

"Hawsie! Hawsie!" Liam shouted and struggled to get down.

Wilson turned to the frazzled mom. "He can pet the horses. Just hold him up so he can touch their necks and shoulders."

The woman nodded, then glanced back at the stroller before she gingerly approached the equines. Liam, on the other hand, was enthusiastically waving his arms and vocalizing.

"I wish I had a picture of this to send to his grandma, but I don't have enough arms."

"Here." Jax motioned her over and held out his hands. "He can sit up here with me, and you can get your photo."

"Thank you so much!" She handed Liam off and went to get her phone from the stroller bag.

Fresh blood seeped from old wounds in Jax's heart. *Would Fallon have been so horse-crazy? She'd be old enough to have her own pony now.* But he kept smiling. "Hey, Liam. This horsie's name is Velvet. Can you say Vel-vet?"

Liam giggled. "Beh beh!"

The phone quacked like a duck with each picture Liam's mother took. Jax kept one arm wrapped around the toddler and gently rubbed Velvet's shoulder with his rein hand. *So proud of you girl. You're doing great.*

The phone stopped quacking, and the woman's brow furrowed. "We've been camping here a bunch of times, and we've never seen cops. Is something wrong?" Her eyes got bigger. "Escaped fugitives or something?"

Wilson shook her head. "No, ma'am. No fugitives. We haven't seen anything suspicious this morning. Have you?"

The woman thought for a moment, then shook her head. "No."

"See? It's all good." Wilson grinned at her. We need to get back so the horses can have their lunch. You have a good rest of your day, ma'am."

Jax handed Liam back to his mother, and he burst into tears. The wailing finally faded into the growing distance between them and the stroller.

As they approached the end of the lake, two figures became visible in the brush on the woods side of the path. One wore a white tee shirt and stood out like a magnesium flare. The one in the olive shirt was hard to see unless he moved. Wilson raised her hand to signal the riders to stop.

"Hey there!" she called to the two men.

They froze.

"Come out here and talk to us for a minute." Her tone was friendly but firm.

The men bolted into the woods. Seconds later, an ATV roared to life. They could see it coming right toward them as it tore out of the woods. This oversized machine was outfitted with a roll bar and a reinforced grill guard with a winch attachment.

Poachermobile. Jax narrowed his eyes.

The ATV raced across the path and into the woods on the other side.

Wilson pointed toward the water. "Jax—you and Jess cut them off!"

She urged her horse into a gallop as she reached for her radio and called for backup.

The fastest way for Jax and Jess to get to the other side of the woods was to cut across the lake. He'd never tried to swim Velvet before. *Hope you like water, girl.*

The mare hesitated at the bank but followed Jess' grey mare into the chilly water. The bottom dropped off suddenly, and both horses were swimming. *I hope there aren't any alligators in here.*

The swim was short, but the footing was deep and sticky on the opposite bank. It was tough going getting out, and the roar of the ATV got louder. They trotted to the road, and Jax could see it, sliding from side to side as it went too fast on the clay path. A noise caught his attention, and he turned to see Liam and his mom coming toward them on the road.

She veered off the main trail onto a side path toward the cabins.

The poachermobile veered off the path to go around the horses.

In seconds, they would collide.

"No!" Jax shouted and spurred Velvet into a canter off the trail.

There was a sickening thud as the ATV hit the horse. Time slowed, and Jax saw trees and sky whirling together.

Falling.

Blackness.

Chapter
Thirty-Four

"IVY!"

Jax?

Ivy jerked awake and sat up, but she was alone in the dark.

She reached for her phone to see what time it was, but the device was a brick.

How long has this been out of battery?

Her e-reader was on the table, so she grabbed it and opened the cover. She'd only overslept fifteen minutes.

Fantastic. I needed more stress on finals day.

She'd taken today off—Tuesday—and her exams were at 9 AM and 11:30 AM. A lunch splurge was in order afterward. But now she had to get a move on to get her barn chores done.

Ivy only had time to hit the highlights, or lowlights, as the case may be, in the shower, and her breakfast was a large cup of coffee. Grateful for programmable coffee makers, she plugged her phone into a lipstick charger, silenced it, and tossed the phone and battery into her purse. She'd check her email later. There was so much crammed into her brain that she couldn't afford to add one more scrap of information, in case it pushed something she needed for her finals out of her head.

She didn't even turn on the radio in the car.

Her statistics final was first. Panic swept through her when she reached into her bag and could not find her calculator.

How am I supposed to do standard deviation in my head?

She pawed through the purse again and found the calculator safely tucked away in one of the inner pockets. *I'm sure I put it there to make it easier to find. Gah!*

Ivy had finished her test and was checking it over for the third time. She clicked 'submit' with a comfortable ten minutes to spare. The results would be posted in a couple of hours.

She might actually have done okay. Now, on to economics.

The second final was not as easy as she'd expected. When it was turned in, her brain felt like a lime Jell-O salad with cottage cheese and walnuts.

I'm free! Until January.

She got in her car and drove the four blocks to "Yo Mamma Said Pho!" The restaurant had only been open a month, but it was the *it* place. Surely, there would be a table open at 1:30 on a Tuesday.

There were actually several tables, and Ivy sat by the window and studied the menu. She finally decided on a veggie pho that was accompanied by a scaffolded salad with exotic greens, carved vegetables, and edible orchids. She wasn't sure if it was a meal or an art installation. Ivy took a long swig of tea.

Now. Time to check my mail.

When she turned the phone on, she found she had four emails, eight texts, and two missed calls. Ivy rolled her eyes.

Wish Margaret would learn how to unjam the copier. It would save everybody at the office a lot of hassle.

Julie had sent a draft copy of a grant application. Ivy tried several times to read it, but her brain was too squishy from her exams, and she felt like she was reading gibberish. *I'll look at that later.*

The next two emails were money requests from one charity she'd never heard of and one political PAC. She deleted both. The last one was from a lady who wanted to come out and look at the horses, with the idea that she might possibly want to volunteer. By the time Ivy hit *send* on her response, her food arrived.

It was even more spectacular than the photo in the menu. She couldn't help herself. Even if the food wasn't amazing, it was profoundly photogenic. She had to take pictures. No one would believe her otherwise. After taking a wide angle and a few closeups of the flowers, she tried the soup. It wasn't bad, but she'd had better. She ate one of the orchids. It was...different. The petals were thick and tasted vaguely of cucumbers. She used her fork to pick some noodles out of the pho broth.

Ivy sighed and looked at the empty chair across from her. She tried to imagine Jax sitting there, as if wishing could make him appear. What would he say about her over-the-top salad? She could picture him tucking a flower behind his ear just to tease her. Why hadn't she just given him a chance to explain? She'd ruined everything, and she couldn't see any way to fix it. She blotted a tear.

No more putting it off. Have to deal with Margaret. She tapped the call log icon on her phone. One of the missed calls was from the mystery number that had come in over the weekend.

The other was from Helen.

Something was wrong. Ivy could feel it in her bones. She hit redial.

"Ivy! Thank God you called. You have to get down here!"

"What?"

"Jax has been in an accident. Horse fell on him. He was life-flighted to Hermann. He's in ICU and...and...we're not sure he's going to make it." Her voice broke.

"I'm on my way." *No! This can't be happening. No. I refuse to believe it.* But a tear streaked down her cheek as she gathered her things.

She hurried to the cashier, tossed the credit card and receipt into her bag, and ran out to her car.

The air in the vehicle must have disappeared, because she could hardly breathe. Her hands trembled so hard she struggled to fit the key into the ignition.

Thwap!

Ivy jumped as the pedestrian she had just nearly backed over slapped the trunk of her car.

"Sorry!" But she didn't take the time to roll down the window, and the angry man likely didn't hear her.

The trip to The Medical Center was a blur. Would Jax make it? Would she get there in time to see him? Hot tears flowed down her cheeks.

I am so stupid. Why didn't I just talk to him? I may never get another chance to say I'm sorry.

221

Ivy had to ask at the Information Desk how to get up to ICU. The croakiness of her voice surprised her.

The icy tightness in the pit of her stomach grew worse as the elevator rose. Ivy wiped her damp palms on her jeans as the doors opened and she stepped out onto the ICU floor. That hospital smell—equal parts disinfectant and despair—almost overwhelmed her as the elevator doors opened. She swallowed hard and followed the signs to the waiting room.

Helen looked up as Ivy came in, and the misery on her face almost broke Ivy's heart. Helen's eyes were red and puffy.

She rose and met Ivy in the middle of the small sitting area. Crushing her into a desperate hug, she whispered in Ivy's ear. "I'm so glad you made it. He's been in and out of consciousness, but he kept calling for you as they were taking him to surgery. Fractured ribs, punctured lung, ruptured spleen. There's a fracture across his pelvis." Helen ran her hand down her face, as if she was trying to wipe away the bad news. "The nurses are in there right now. I'll take you in when they come out."

A boulder-sized lump grew in Ivy's throat. "What happened?"

Helen told her about the campground thieves and the ATV. How Jax had gotten in between the toddler and the bad guys.

Oh, god. Poor Ruby.

A woman and a man, both in scrubs, came into the waiting area. Helen pulled Ivy over to them.

The woman shifted a small tablet computer in her hands. "He's still critical, but he is stable, and his vitals are good, considering. He's still sedated and on the ventilator. He can hear you, so talk to him. Just don't expect him to answer and don't feel bad if he doesn't remember. You can go back in now, no more than two at a time."

Ivy couldn't stop the tear that rolled down her cheek and dripped off her chin.

Helen led her to the ICU ward. The desk nurse stopped them. "Sorry, Ms. Butterfield. Immediate family only. You know the rules."

"But she's his fiancée. Surely that counts?"

Ivy felt blood rush to her cheeks. *Some fiancée. Jax might not even be speaking to me.*

The nurse raised an eyebrow.

"Her name is Ivy. You heard him calling for her before...before...."

"Fine." The nurse exhaled loudly. "Fifteen minutes. No more."

"Thank you!"

Ivy knew that Jax had been in an accident, but she wasn't prepared for what she saw. He lay in the bed, a sheet and blanket pulled up to his waist. Purple bruises and angry red scrapes stood out against his too-pale skin. She could see the top of a surgical dressing peeking out from under the sheet. Machines beeped and whirred. The lower half of his face was mostly hidden by tubes and tape. An IV tube snaked up from his arm to yet another machine.

Helen gestured to the only chair near Jax's bed, and Ivy sat in it. She reached out to touch his face, but stopped, afraid she would hurt him.

His sister must have seen the hesitation. "He's on a lot of pain medication. I don't think he'll feel anything."

"Hey, Jax." Ivy breathed deeply and slowly trying to straighten out the quiver in her voice. Her fingers lightly caressed his forehead. "You're doing great. Please. Please come back to us. We all miss you so much. I'm sorry I screwed up. You have to wake up so I can make it up to you."

Ivy couldn't choke back her tears any longer, so she stopped talking. But she held his hand.

Helen stood on the other side of the bed. "Ajax. Little brother. Who's going to take care of Flip if you don't get back here?"

She leaned over and sang softly near Jax's ear. Ivy couldn't make out the words, but it sounded like a children's song, or maybe a lullaby.

It seemed hardly any time at all had passed when the nurse stuck her head in and tapped her watch. Ivy nodded and stood up. Helen finished her song, then whispered in Jax's ear before she rose and turned toward the door.

Ivy didn't go into the waiting area. "Helen, I have to go take care of the horses. Please text me if anything changes. I don't care what time it is. I'll come by after work tomorrow."

"I'm so glad you came."

The elevator made some alarming sounds on its way down but reached the ground floor successfully. She saw

Lieutenant Wilson striding across the lobby toward the elevator. Jax's boss looked like she hadn't slept in days.

"Ivy? How's he doing?"

"The nurse said he's stable."

Wilson nodded absently. "That's good. It was touch and go last night during the surgery."

If only I had known! "Lieutenant? I just wanted to say how sorry I am about Ruby."

"Ruby? She's fine. He was on...." Wilson's eyes widened. "Velvet. I'm real sorry, Ivy. I should have called you, but—"

Ivy couldn't stand to hear any more. She held up her hands as if to physically block Wilson's words and fled.

Chapter
Thirty-Five

JAX OPENED HIS eyes, but the glare of the midafternoon sun made his head hurt, so he kept them closed. He groaned as someone removed his helmet.

"Leave the Kevlar."

Who said that? He knew the voice but had trouble placing it.

Jax curled the fingers of his right hand, just to see if he could, and moved his arm away from his body a few inches. His hand brushed something warm. Hair. Short Not fur. Not human. Velvet.

This can't be good. He tried to sit up, but pain roared through his body, and he collapsed limply into the grass.

Someone leaned over him. "Easy there, Jax. Help is on the way. You're going to be fine. Just be still." That voice again. He knew her, believed her. Still, he tried to talk.

"V-v-v..."

"Don't worry about Velvet. We'll take care of her. You concentrate on you."

Quack! Quack!

The woman leaning over him rose and he could hear her take a few steps away.

"Dr. Leventhal?...Yes...Dr. Mueller is on the way...Can you arrange transport?...Okay...Okay...Thank you."

Jax reached out for Velvet again. *Stay with me.*

He felt like he was floating, gazing out into the heart of the Milky Way. Stars shimmered all around him, even as deep space apparently smelled like dead grass and black gumbo.

It was hardly noticeable at first, but he could feel it long before he heard it.

Thumpthumpthumpthump!

The throbbing shockwave of the chopper's rotor echoed in his chest as it approached. The noise was almost unbearable when it got close. He just wanted to sleep.

He drifted.

Equipment clattered.

People shouted.

Words floated over him. *Shock. Ringers Lactate. Internal injuries.*

He almost cried out in pain as he was lifted just enough for EMS to slide a backboard underneath him. Moving hurt. Moving was bad. The backboard was lifted, and he was strapped onto a stretcher.

Blackness.

When he drifted up from the depths of unconsciousness again, the gurney was rolling down a hospital corridor. *Where is Ivy? She has to be here.* He needed her to come help him. People were running. They pushed him into a room. The lights were too bright. He closed his eyes. Someone put something over his face.

Blackness.

And then he was walking down a dirt road in the country. The sun was halfway up the horizon and low fog floated over the pale green grass. Jax shivered. Caliche crunched under his feet. His shoes were soaked with chilly dew from the tall grass along the road. The air smelled like spring. The crisp edge of distant snows had mostly faded into the round smell of warming earth and waking plants. A few birds twittered in the trees to his right, but he didn't see them.

It felt like he walked for hours without seeing another soul. Finally, he saw a bay horse grazing in the misty meadow. It raised its head and regarded him for a moment, then whinnied as it trotted toward him.

No. It can't be. Murphy?

The horse stopped a dozen or so yards away and nickered. Jax broke into a run. In spite of that, he didn't get any closer to the horse. He looked down, to make sure he wasn't on a treadmill, but the pale gravel kept its secrets.

"Murphy!" he called. The horse whinnied in response, but didn't get any closer.

Jax gave up trying to approach his horse and stood still. Far behind the equine, he noticed a figure, silhouetted against the rising sun. He watched as the breeze played with her hair and tugged at the hem of her skirt. It hurt to breathe. Jax felt like his insides were being pulled out. There was no mistaking the identity of the woman approaching him.

Elise.

She stood next to Murphy. Jax tried to run to her but could get nowhere. He had missed her so much for so long. It was pure anguish not to be able to sweep her into his arms and crush her against him. Instead, he stared at her face.

Long black hair framed her features, and her hazel-green eyes sparkled as she looked back at him.

Suddenly, the barrier broke, and Jax stumbled forward. He caught Elise in his arms, holding her while he struggled to contain his emotions. Finally, she pushed away from him.

Jax reached out and stroked Murphy's neck as he looked around. "Where's Fallon?"

"She isn't here. She has a new mommy now."

"I don't understand."

"She had to go back. She wasn't finished. But they gave me a message for you. It's your choice. You can go back, or you can stay here. Whichever you want."

The choice seemed obvious. He shivered again. Why was he so cold?

And then he heard another voice. One that he had so hoped to hear only a short time ago. Ivy's voice.

"Please. Please come back to us."

Chapter
Thirty-Six

IVY SAT NEXT to Jax's bed. She'd come by every day after work. There had been no change all week, between the internal injuries, sedation, and pain medication. Now it was a chilly, rainy Saturday afternoon, and he still lay motionless in the bed. She held his hand and talked to him about whatever came off the top of her head—Silver, Amos, her finals, *Yo Mama Said Pho*, and Flip.

"You know, Helen asked me to take care of Flip while you're laid up. He's getting along great with Twilight and Eddie, but especially Flash. He misses you, though. I can tell. He gets so excited when I come home from the hospital—he can smell you on me, I'm sure."

Helen paused her crochet. "Flip's in good hands, but he needs you."

Ivy didn't dare mention Velvet, or Styx, either—she wouldn't be able to talk.

She wasn't sure at first that she'd felt it, so she held her breath. Helen noticed.

There it was again. A twitch. Pressure. Ever so slightly, Jax squeezed her hand.

Helen's crochet hook clattered to the floor. "Did he...?"

"Yes!"

Jax's eyelashes fluttered, and he squinted against the fluorescent lights.

"He's awake!" Helen punched the call button on the bedside remote.

"How can I help you?" a female voice crackled out of the tinny speaker.

"My brother! He woke up!"

"I'll get the doctor."

It wasn't long before the doctor swept into the room, flanked by a nurse and a resident. They shooed Ivy and Helen out of the room.

Jax was discharged after ten long days. Ivy sat in the patient pickup drive-through, craning her neck each time the door opened to see if it was him. Finally, the nurse pushed his wheelchair through the automatic glass doors. Ivy practically leaped out of the car to open the door and stow the big bag 'o discharge papers and whatnot in the back seat.

He flinched as he slid into the passenger seat. Ivy hated that he was in pain. Still, it was good to be sitting next to him, no IVs, no beeping machines. She wasn't about to waste her second chance. "You okay?"

"Yeah. Only hurts when I breathe."

"Well, just don't... oh. Are you going to be able to get up the steps?"

"There's only four of them. I think I can manage." Jax buckled his seatbelt. "What did you tell your boss?"

"I don't have to justify my vacation. Besides, I have al-most two weeks left and if I don't use 'em this month, I'll lose 'em." Ivy waited for a car to creep past before she pulled away from the curb.

"You don't have to do this. I'm glad that you are, don't get me wrong. But...."

"Jax, you can't stay home alone. Helen bought you a fancy recliner—it arrived yesterday. It'll even push you out of the seat, if you need it to."

"I always wanted a grandpa chair," he grumbled.

Jax stared out the window for a while. When they passed a shopping plaza that was mostly restaurants, he coughed. "I'm sorry you didn't get one of the grants at the gala."

Ivy was mostly focused on waiting for an opening in traffic to make a turn. "Yeah. It's not the end of the world, but it sure would have helped."

"I might be able to help."

"No, Jax. You earned that money for Bookstar. Those kids deserve it."

His breathing was shallow. "Not what I meant. Had Thanksgiving with my brother-in-law's mother. She's decided to give all of her money to charity, and she's already handing out grants."

"Really? I mean...that would be amazing."

"She had a website set up." His lips pressed together in pain. "I'll put in a word for you."

"That sounds great, but let's worry about that later, okay? You just rest."

There wasn't a lot of conversation on the drive back to Ivy's house. She knew every breath brought searing pain, so she didn't want him to talk unless it was absolutely necessary. The dogs in the house barked loud enough for Ivy to hear them as she pulled up the driveway.

Ivy helped Jax out of her car and up the steps. She made sure he had a drink and some snacks, then stepped out to feed the horses. When she came back, he'd fallen asleep. He looked so peaceful. She longed to touch him, but didn't dare, in case she woke him up. Ivy smiled, her heart full.

Ivy set her iced tea on the end table. "Jax are you sure about this? You've only been out of the hospital a week."

"I know. Styx has probably grown an inch or two since the last time I laid eyes on him. I just need to go see him."

Ivy gave him half a smile. "Me, too."

Ivy handed Jax his crutches. Going up and down the stairs was still a struggle, but he was healing fast, all things considered. His clothes sagged on him, and a flabby sweatpants pocket caught on the door handle, nearly sending him sprawling. The rubber foot of the crutch made an impressive *thunk* on the wooden porch as he caught his balance.

"Careful."

"I'm not a baby!" Jax snapped.

"Never said you were." Ivy opened the car door, and he eased himself inside.

She stowed the crutches in the back seat before she got in and started the car. They were almost twenty minutes into the trip to the police stables before either of them said a word.

"I'm sorry." Jax sighed. "I feel so damned helpless. I hate it. I really do appreciate everything you're doing for me."

"I'm sorry, too. When I read that letter, I just assumed... I should have let you explain. And then when Helen sent me the picture of the headstone. I realized I'd been so stupid, and thought you'd never speak to me again."

Jax reached over to the center console and caressed her hand.

The silence grew less comfortable as the miles slid by.

Jax exhaled deeply. "I still can't remember what happened. I recall looking for you after the gala, but you'd already left. Then I woke up in a hospital bed with you and Helen in my room."

"It's probably for the best. I wouldn't want to remember...."

Too many bad memories already troubled Jax's sleep, even after all this time. "I think you're right."

The driveway to the police stables was coming up. Ivy swallowed hard and her eyelashes were suddenly wet.

The thought of orphaned Styx in Velvet's empty paddock was almost too much to bear.

I VY PULLED INTO a parking spot near the door. Jax undid his seat belt but made no move to open the door.

"The empty halter is the hardest part, isn't it?" Ivy squeezed his hand.

"Yeah." Jax reached for the door handle. "The LT said to find her first."

Unbuckling her own seatbelt, Ivy got out and hurried to the passenger side to get Jax's crutches. She walked beside him as he hobbled along, longing to see Styx but dreading his mother's absence. If Jax wanted, she could bring the colt back to the rescue. Now that Copper Penny was receiving a generous monthly sponsorship from Irene's charitable foundation, Ivy could take in a dozen orphan foals.

The receptionist buzzed them in. "Jax! How are you feeling?"

"Like I got hit by a truck, but other than that, I'm fine."

"But you did. well, I guess it was a Gator, but still. Lieutenant Wilson's in her office."

The rubber tips on the crutches squeaked with each step on the tile floor.

Was this hallway always this long? Ivy followed Jax on his slow progression. It almost felt like a doomed trip to the gallows, even though Jax had done nothing wrong. She'd been told that Jax had saved a mother and a baby. But sacrificed Velvet. She'd known, on some level, that being a police horse was not without risk. It had seemed like an abstraction, something that might happen to someone else.

Lt. Wilson's door was open. A thirty-something man sat across the desk from her. His black wavy hair fell into his blue eyes when he stood up.

The lieutenant also got to her feet. "Jax. Ivy. This is Dr. Berringer. He's from the vet school at A & M."

Jax leaned on his crutch and extended his forearm. "Professor or student?"

The doctor blinked. "Neither actually." -

"Why don't we head out to the paddocks?" Lt. Wilson broke in.

Ivy's stomach knotted itself. She had to back up so the others could get out of Lt. Wilson's office.

She nodded. "Everything considered, Jax, you look pretty damn good.

"Thanks."

Ivy stood close enough to him that she heard the intake of breath, as if he planned to say something else, but didn't.

The noise barely registered at first. It sounded like a power tool or mechanical device. Building getting a new roof, maybe?

Ka-choonk. Ka-choonk. Ka-choonk.

The noise got louder as they cut through the tack room to the barn aisle. Styx's high-pitched whinny carried over the sound, then it stopped.

Ivy reached into her jacket pocket and pulled out the remains of the bag of soft molasses treats. They should be soft enough for him to eat—and they'd been Velvet's favorite. In a way, he'd been eating them before he was born.

At the sound of the crinkling bag, a horse nickered. A deep, throaty chuckle.

Jax and Ivy looked at each other.

He cocked his head. "That sounds like—"

"Velvet." Ivy finished his sentence, wanting to shove the lieutenant and doctor out of the way to see why she was hearing something she could not possibly be hearing.

Jax stepped through the doorway and gasped. Ivy looked at him, then at the aisleway. There in the crossties stood a horse.

A black and white draft cross.

With one blue eye and one brown.

Velvet stamped a back foot. *Ka-choonk.*

Jax and Ivy hurried to the horse. Ivy gave her a treat before studying the mare. Her hind legs were encased in maroon lattices. What looked like scaffolding with wires and black boxes wrapped around each of her hind legs, all the way up and connecting over her rump.

Ivy rubbed Velvet's nose and gave her another cookie. She threw her arms around the mare's neck and buried her face in Velvet's thick mane, inhaling the horsey smell that is almost like a drug among riders. When she pulled away, Velvet's neck had two damp spots. Ivy wiped the horse hair from her eyes.

Styx trotted up, demanding his own treat.

Jax stroked Velvet's shoulder. "I don't understand."

Dr. Berringer cleared his throat. "I can explain. Horses are perfectly capable of healing broken bones. They do it all the time. The problem is when it's a leg bone, movement is terrible for bone healing. But if you keep the horse immobile, their feet fall apart. Literally. My company builds robots, specifically biomechanical exoskeletons, to help people with mobility issues. We've recently started working with the veterinary college to see if we could help animals, too." He leaned over and touched the maroon lattice. "This is a custom 3D printed cast to keep her bones stable." He laid his hand on the scaffolding. "This is the exoskeleton. It supports her weight so she can move around and keep her hooves healthy."

"How long will she have to wear that?" Ivy scratched Styx under his curly baby mane.

"We're taking X-rays every week. The bone appears to be healing well. After six to eight weeks, we'll start decreasing the amount of support she gets from the exoskeleton. Once that gets down to zero, we'll take it and the casts off, and she should be good as new."

Jax turned to Lt. Wilson. "Why didn't you tell me this?"

She gave him half a smile. "It's an experimental procedure. Still 50-50 whether it will work. You already thought she was dead. I didn't want to get your hopes up, in case it failed."

"Well, now that she's gotten used to the exo, I think the odds are significantly better," Dr. Berringer chimed in.

"Ivy, would you mind putting Velvet away? Alphonse'll be out with their grain soon." Lt. Wilson gave Ivy a nod.

"Of course!" Ivy picked up the lead rope that had been draped over the horse's neck and unclipped her from the crossties. Her heart felt so warm and light that it would float away if it wasn't contained within her chest. So much joy surged through her body that it almost hurt.

Ka-choonk. Ka-choonk. Ka-choonk.

One of the best sounds Ivy had ever heard. She led the big mare into her stall, Styx following with his fluffy tail in the air and squealing. Velvet went straight to her hay. Styx sidled up to his dam and started nursing. Ivy took the mare's halter off and walked out.

Jax took it from her and hung it on the hook by Velvet's nameplate. "I'd never have believed this if I hadn't seen it."

Ivy couldn't help the tear that trickled down her cheek as she reached for Jax's hand. He interlaced his warm fingers with hers as they watched the horses eat. For the first time in a long time, she was happy. Truly happy.

Jax squeezed her hand. "Penny for your thoughts."

"Oh... I was just thinking that Velvet gets a second second chance, and Styx isn't an orphan. I get a second chance with you."

Jax turned to face her. He put one crutch forward for balance, then bent his head to kiss her.

She closed her eyes and would have melted into his arms, if he'd been able to hold her. When he pulled away from the kiss, he rested his forehead on hers for a moment. He looked into her eyes and the world seemed to dissolve around them.

"Ivy Stonewall, I love you."

Her breath caught in her chest, and she couldn't speak. It felt like minutes passed before she was able to push out the words, "I love you, too."

"I know." Jax leaned in to kiss her again.

A flurry of whinnies, knickers, and snorts erupted from the far end of the barn, and the wave of sound rolled down both sides of the aisle.

Alphonse had appeared with a cart laden with buckets of grain. He waved to Jax and Ivy. They sheepishly waved back.

Jax brushed her hair out of her eyes. "Let's go home."

Home. She liked that word, so laden with meaning, chock-full of happiness and comfort. "Yes. I'd go anywhere with you. But home sounds best."

If you enjoyed this book, please consider leaving a review at your favorite book site. Reviews help other readers find and enjoy new books!

To explore more content from Coda Sterling, visit BlackMareBooks.com